UNDER THE SURFACE

BEAR & MANDY LOGAN BOOK TWO

L.T. RYAN

with

K.M. ROUGHT

LIQUID MIND MEDIA

THE BEAR & MANDY LOGAN SERIES

Close to Home

Under the Surface

The Last Stop

Over the Edge

Between the Lies (Coming Soon)

Love Bear? Mandy? Noble? Hatch? Get your very own L.T. Ryan merchandise today! Click the link below to find coffee mugs, t-shirts, and even signed copies of your favorite thrillers! https://ltryan.ink/EvG_

1

LUIS WIPED AWAY A BEAD OF SWEAT THREATENING TO TRICKLE INTO HIS left eye. He needed all his focus for what would happen next. They'd come too far to screw it up now. One more day until he'd finally be safe. And rich.

Next to him, Marco leaned forward and tapped the portable satnav device they'd duct taped to the rickety submarine's wall. Every movement sent a whiff of something or other through the vessel. The other man's body odor. Human waste from the bucket in the corner. Stale breath so acrid, it nearly brought tears to Luis' eyes.

"Time?" Marco asked. A Mexican man, his words rolled off the tongue in ways different from Luis'. How he'd ended up in Colombia was anyone's guess. Luis hadn't cared enough to ask. "Pay attention."

Luis looked down at the paper map in his hands so Marco wouldn't see the anger in his eyes.

Time? Time? Time? Luis had forced himself not to count how many times a day Marco had asked him that. It had to be well into the triple-digits. There was little else to do on the sub other than check the map and count down every excruciating second as it passed. "Four hours. A little less."

Marco nodded, as though he'd confirmed what they'd both already known. "Last trip to the surface. Make it count."

Luis folded the map and tucked it under the pillow on his cot. The cramped space wasn't much of an issue—he'd grown up poor, with five siblings—but the inability to stand to his full height was wearing on him. He wanted to straighten his back. Stretch his legs. Get away from Marco, at least for a few minutes a day. Even sleeping didn't help. Not when Marco woke him every few hours, grunting or groaning or snoring like he'd inhaled a chainsaw.

Luis had made this trip twice before, but he'd never get used to the conditions. The sub was hot and stale and liable to collapse on them at any moment. They had enough food for both of them, but Marco always somehow ended up with more. And having to listen to the man shit in front of him turned Luis' stomach, even if he'd never say so.

Worst of all was driving blind. There were two windows built into the cockpit just below the hatch, but he might as well have been trying to look out two toilet paper rolls taped together. He could just about see what was right in front of him, but problems rarely came head on.

Experience had not abated the fears. In fact, it had done the exact opposite. They had their location in the open ocean, but the homemade sub had no radar. They'd painted the outside of their craft blue so they could stay close to the surface and avoid detection, but closer to the coast meant shallower water.

As they inched toward the shoals, they had to be twice as careful. Animals weren't so much of a problem. The sub was six meters long—too big and unappetizing for most predators. And the ones who were interested usually shoved them around for a minute or two before deciding they weren't food.

No, the bigger problem was the debris. This close to the North Carolina coast, the ocean floor was littered with shipwrecks. They could plot that route as much as they wanted, but the shifting sands and crashing waves unearthed long-buried secrets sooner or later. If they ran into something much bigger than them, they wouldn't likely come out the victor. Even if they did survive, losing their cargo was a death sentence.

After surviving his first trip, Luis had promised himself he wouldn't do it again. A month later, he was back out in the open ocean. The money was too good. A couple weeks' worth of hell was enough to put food on the table for months at a time. The look on his kids' faces when he had returned with armfuls of groceries had been worth it. Even his wife, with that suspicious look in her eyes, couldn't say no to their new and improved life.

But this really was his final trip. He'd paid down his debts. He was a free man. This would be all profit. Enough to pack up his family and leave for good. Find a decent job. Start living the life he'd always wanted. He'd never have to see that look in his wife's eyes again.

"Pay attention," Marco barked. His second favorite phrase. "Get ready."

Getting ready meant taking two steps to reach the other side of the room and grabbing the handle on the waste bucket. He held his breath but still tasted it in his mouth. Four hours wasn't soon enough.

Marco stepped over to the cockpit. Bigger subs had separate rooms for navigation and steering equipment. Still cramped, but more state-of-the-art than this one. At least, as state-of-the-art as you could get when you had to build your ship in the jungle and sneak it out to sea.

It didn't take long to breach the surface. Luis didn't even feel a difference in pressure. He closed his eyes and took a deep breath as soon as Marco opened the hatch. He had never cared for the ocean, but now he was sure the salt air was one of the most refreshing smells on the planet. It beat fresh crap, anyway.

Marco stuck his head out of the hatch and did a full three-sixty. "Clear," he said before hauling himself through the opening. "It's windy."

Out of Marco's view, Luis rolled his eyes. It was always windy. And he'd done this enough to know not to throw the contents of the bucket into the wind. That made for a miserable trip.

With one hand steadying the bucket, Luis hauled himself through the opening high enough to sit and scoot backwards, straddling the craft between his legs. The metal was still cool, but it wouldn't take long to heat up under the afternoon sun. Not on a day as clear as this one.

Despite Marco's all-clear, Luis did a sweep himself. It's not that he didn't trust the man—well, he didn't—but it was always better to have a second set of eyes on the horizon. The Coast Guard or some naval ship could appear out of nowhere. In which case, they'd be screwed. There was no denying the white bricks below deck were anything but cocaine, and no one from back home was stupid enough to bail them out of jail. He might be able to get a plea deal if he offered to turn in the guys running the operation, but his wife and kids would be dead before he ever had the chance to set foot back on Colombian soil.

No, better to just not get caught in the first place. Luckily for him, Marco was smart. Once of the first runners to take to the sea, and he'd been training people ever since. Part of Luis wondered if he'd ever been friendly, but the other part didn't care past this moment because once they were done, he was gone.

Luis shifted to one side and dumped the contents of the bucket into the sea. He always wondered if it attracted any marine life or scared them away. Did it smell as bad to them? Could they get any nutrients from it? He didn't know a single thing about marine biology, and as he thought about it more, he didn't think he would ever bother learning.

Marco grunted at him. "Clean it out good."

Luis ground his teeth together to stop himself from saying something he regretted. He leaned over and used the ocean to rinse out the bucket. Something stuck to the bottom of the metal can, and he wished he at least had a brush. There was no way he was touching that with his hand.

A slight vibration went through the sub. Luis looked back at Marco, who was staring at him. "That you?"

"No." Luis looked down at the hunk of metal underneath him. "What was that?"

"Could've been a shark." Marco stood up, having no problem balancing atop the rocking craft. "I'll take a look."

Luis drew his feet back until he was kneeling. His sea legs weren't as seasoned as Marco's, and he didn't want to risk tumbling overboard. Not with a shark potentially circling them. He couldn't see anything other than a few curious fish a couple feet down. That didn't mean something else wasn't there.

"Crawl over to the other end. Look off the back," Marco instructed.

Luis swished water through the bucket one more time, but whatever was stuck to the bottom refused to let go. He dropped the pail through the hatch and froze when he heard a splash.

"We're taking on water." Luis' voice was devoid of any emotion. He was still trying to comprehend the severity. "There's a good couple inches down there already."

"Piece of shit," Marco said. Luis didn't know if the man was talking about him or the sub. "Move."

Luis had to scratch at the metal to stay on top of the sub while Marco shoved him out of the way. The older man dropped through the hole, cursing as soon as he splashed down. The water was coming in fast.

"What happened?" Luis asked.

"How the hell should I know," Marco said, as though it was Luis' fault they were sinking. "Piece of shit welders, probably. We need to find the hole."

That was easier said than done. The cargo hold was full of bricks, packed as tightly as they could get them. A literal ton of cocaine weighed them down. If they hit the bottom of the ocean this far from the coast, they would stay there. Eventually someone would come to rescue the cargo, but they'd be long dead.

Marco must've had the same thought. "We need to lose some weight." He tossed a pillow into Luis' face. "And gun it to the coast. We can make it if we're fast."

Luis tossed the pillow into the ocean. "There's not much to toss." *Except the cargo*, he thought. That would never happen. They'd both be dead if there was even an ounce missing. "We're not going to make it."

Marco ignored him. He tossed up another pillow, plus their blankets. Then folded the mattresses in half and shoved them through the opening. Luis pushed them overboard and watched as they sank to the bottom of the ocean. One day, someone might find it and wonder how a whole bed had gotten lost at sea.

Marco grabbed the tiny folding table that they used for card games. He snapped that in half and passed the pieces to Luis, who chucked them. Then Marco disappeared. The sub shuddered, then stabilized. The other man must've dumped some of their excess fuel. It was a risk, but what other option did they have? Marco would toss Luis overboard before he ever considered chucking the cocaine through the hatch.

Marco must've had the same thought because one moment he was searching for something else he could pull off the wall of the sub, and the next minute he was launching himself through the hatch and burying a knife in Luis' chest.

"It's not personal," Marco said.

It felt personal. One minute he was sitting on top of the sub, the metal finally warming in the sun, and the next he was sinking through the water, wondering which would come first—bleeding out, drowning, or becoming shark food.

2

BEAR STARED UP AT THE CEILING IN THE FIRST-FLOOR BATHROOM, watching water drip into a bucket from its upstairs counterpart. It came down slow enough that it wouldn't fill the pail for another two or three days, but it was steady. The leak would just get worse. He itched to fix it himself.

Not your house. Not your problem.

He'd kept that mantra alive over the last few months, refusing to go out of his way to repair the issues that seemed to double or triple on a daily basis. Peeling paint and rotting floorboards had been enough of a shock when they'd walked through the door, but at this point, those were the least of his worries. He'd already fixed a broken toilet and replaced the kitchen faucet out of necessity. Now he regretted giving the owner his time and money for free.

This had been one of the few affordable houses left in Cape Hatteras. The population always shrank around this time—January was the coldest month, though usually above freezing—but every other rental property had been booked solid through the rest of the Spring. He and Mandy had been lucky. Or so he'd thought.

Now, staring up at the water dripping from the ceiling, he was pretty sure they were cursed. Maybe karma finally caught up to him. He always thought he'd go out with a bullet in the back of his head, not wasting away from insanity.

There was an easy solution to this. Show up at the owner's doorstep and use his considerable height to make the guy do the bare minimum. But the owner wasn't on the island. And he wasn't answering his phone or emails. Bear thought about pulling some strings and tracking the guy down, but he already had his hands full.

The front door opened and slammed shut a second later.

Speak of the devil.

Bear turned his back on the bucket, closing the door behind him. By the time he reached the living room, Mandy had already dumped her bag on the ground, kicked her feet up on the couch, and had her phone out, swiping through some social media app. Facebook? Twitter? Instagram? They all looked the same to him.

"I'd recommend using the master bath for your toilet needs." Bear sank down into the recliner opposite Mandy. "Unless you want to pee and shower at the same time."

"Who wouldn't want that?"

"Hey, don't knock it till you try it."

Mandy sighed in response.

"How was school?"

"How do you think?"

"Are you going to answer every question with a question?"

"Do you think I should?"

"If you want to eat liver, cabbage, and SPAM for dinner, then yes."

Mandy twisted around on the couch, placing her feet on the floor and setting her phone on the cushion next to her. She plastered a huge smile on her face. "I had a wonderful day at school today, Bear. Thank you for asking! How was your day?"

"Could've been better." Bear chuckled. "See? Was that so hard?"

"It was excruciating."

"Good. I live to torture you." He leveled her with a look. "Real answers now."

Mandy groaned and let her head fall back. "Why are we here, Bear?"

"That's another question."

It was Mandy's turn to level him with a look, but at least she didn't put on the fake smile this time. "It's terrible. I have one friend in the entire school. Everyone hates me. Classes are hard." She kicked at her backpack, but it was so full of books, it barely moved. "I don't know why I have to learn this shit. It's not going to help me later on."

"Oh no? Why's that?"

"In what reality would I need to know anything about *Shakespeare?*" She said his name like it was a dirty word. "That doesn't count as a question. I'd really like to know."

"If you became a teacher. Or a novelist. Or a film critic."

"I'm not becoming a *teacher*, Bear." She let her head fall back again. "Or a novelist."

"What about a film critic?"

"Maybe horror movies."

"That would be cool. Doubt it pays well, though."

"I'll probably just end up working for the government. Or becoming a contract killer. At least there's money in that."

"Or CEO of a tech startup. You've got options." Bear wasn't ready to talk about Mandy's future and the possibility she could walk in his footsteps. "And I doubt everyone at school hates you."

An unhinged laugh came out of Mandy's mouth. "You're not there, Bear. They've made it very clear."

"Is someone giving you trouble?"

"Nothing I can't handle."

Bear's chest tightened. "We talked about this. If you have a problem—"

"Go to a teacher, yeah." She lowered her voice into a mockery of Bear's gruffness. "No fighting, Mandy. There are other ways to solve your problems." Her voice returned to normal. "I seem to remember you solving a lot of problems with violence, Bear."

"Your job is to be better than me."

"Well, that won't be too hard." Mandy lifted her head and looked at him, her eyebrows pinched together. "I didn't mean that."

"I know." It hurt to hear her say it, though. "This place isn't so bad, if you give it a chance."

"I've tried." She was whining now. "I gave it a chance for a whole day. I'm done with the chances. There's nothing to do here. It's boring and the people are stupid and I'm tired of the ocean."

"Already? Ocean's a pretty big place. There are a lot of cool things out there."

"Doubt it. Once you've seen one drop of water, you've seen them all."

Bear snorted. "Believe it or not, I was a kid once, too."

Mandy gasped but didn't raise her head off the couch. He could see her hand inching closer to her phone.

That settled it. He stood. "Come on. Get up."

"What? Why?" She looked panicked now. "Where are we going?"

"I want to show you something."

3

BEAR LICKED THE SALT FROM HIS LIPS AND FELT THE COOL AIR STING FOR A moment. He raised a hand to greet the elderly couple next door as he steered Mandy toward their destination. Muriel and Joseph Murray were well into their eighties, but they had bright eyes and plenty of stories. They weren't scared of Bear. On the contrary.

"Good afternoon, Mr. Logan." Joseph beamed at him with a mischievous look in his eye. "Dining room light keeps flickering. Think you can take a look at it tomorrow?"

Muriel swatted her husband's arm. "Say hi to the man before you rope him into another project."

Joseph grabbed his arm dramatically. "I said 'good afternoon.' What more to do you want?"

"At least let him say it back, then."

Bear chuckled and came to a stop in front of their house. "Afternoon. Yeah, I can take a look at that light. Not a problem."

"See? The man appreciates my directness. Said so himself."

"That I did, sir."

"Hello, Mandy." Muriel smiled sweetly at the girl from her chair atop the porch. "How's school going?"

"Hello, Mrs. Murray." Mandy's voice was sweet but genuine. "It's going well, thank you. How's your scarf coming along?"

Muriel held up a crochet needle Bear hadn't noticed resting in her lap. "About halfway there. Should be done by tomorrow."

"Where're you two off to?" Joseph asked.

Muriel clicked her tongue. "Dear, don't pry."

He eyed her for a moment. "There's a different between prying and politely inquiring as to one's comings and goings, isn't there, son?"

"It's true." Bear had to stifle a laugh when Muriel threw him a dirty look for his betrayal. These two probably invented the phrase *fights like an old married couple* but the love was there. He felt it every time he was in the same room as them. It made his chest hurt. "Giving Mandy a little history lesson today."

"Good man," Joseph said. "Lots of history to be learned around here. You listen to your father, honey. He knows what he's talking about."

Mandy straightened her shoulders the tiniest bit. "Yes, sir."

"Muriel's making pot pie tonight," Joseph said. "You won't want to miss it."

"Wouldn't dream of it," Bear replied.

With that, he excused the two of them with a polite wave and kept walking down the street. It had taken all of three days for Muriel to introduce herself and get as much information out of Bear as he was willing to part with. The cookies didn't hurt. Helping them around the house kept him busy during the day while Mandy was at school. He had refused monetary compensation, but he couldn't say no to the home-cooked meals. It was one less thing to worry about, and he'd noticed Mandy eating more at dinner now.

They continued down the street lined with coastal homes of all shapes and sizes and styles on either side. Nothing cookie-cutter about it. Once they were out of earshot, Bear looked over at Mandy. "You actually like the Murrays?"

"You'd have to be a monster not to like the Murrays," she said. "Doesn't mean I don't still hate it here. And doesn't explain why we're here in the first place."

Bear was silent for a block, paying attention to the cool breeze blowing his shirt back. The sky was clearer than any other night since they'd been there. "When I was a kid, my parents would bring us here every summer. The day school was out, they'd pack us up in the car, hop on the interstate, and head for Hatteras. Every summer since the first time I can remember."

"That was, like, what? A hundred years ago?"

"A hundred and fifty, actually." Bear bumped her with his hip and she went stumbling, bringing a smile to both their faces.

"You big goon."

He waved her off. "My parents had a house here. Not a big one. It was always falling apart, but it was a roof over our head. We were barely under it, anyway. I had friends—"

Mandy gasped and grabbed his wrist with one hand while clutching her heart with the other. "You had friends?"

"—that I'd meet up with every summer. Bobby, Joey, and Maria. This kid we called Bottle Cap."

"Bottle cap?" Mandy screwed up her face. "Why?"

"Really thick glasses." The memory brought another smile to his face. "We'd meet up on the first day of summer and hang out every minute we could. This place felt like another world. There's so much to explore here. So much to learn."

"Ugh, learning."

"Beats Shakespeare."

"See? Told you Shakespeare is the worst."

"I just want you to give it a chance." Bear felt that familiar pain in his chest. The one that told him to keep his emotions in check, to hide away any vulnerabilities. Any weaknesses. Even from his daughter. "It would mean a lot to me."

"I'm trying, Bear." Mandy's voice was quiet. Contemplative. "Really. It's just hard."

"I know. It's not easy starting over. I've got the benefit of nostalgia. And old age."

"So old," Mandy sang.

"We're not staying forever. But I wanted to show you this place. I wanted—" Bear looked up and his words died in his throat. "What the hell?"

Mandy followed his gaze. One eyebrow rose in response to the scene in front of them. "Is that your old house?"

Bear nodded. He expected to see the small cream-colored house looking a little worse for wear. His parents had bought it in the early eighties and sold it sometime in the late nineties, and he had no idea who'd been living in it since. But he doubted anyone would have been as meticulous about the upkeep as his father.

He hadn't expected to see half a dozen people hauling furniture, boxes, and miscellaneous items into the back of a large moving van. The house looked surprisingly well-kept. Had probably had some work done on it in the intervening years. But the family didn't look happy to be moving. Not that it was ever a fun time, but the kids weren't even running around screaming and driving their parents mad. The whole scene looked out of place.

Bear didn't realize he'd stopped to stare until one of the men paused with a box halfway to the trailer, where a teenage boy about Mandy's age was ready to receive it. "Can I help you?" the man asked. His voice was guarded, and he was looking Bear up and down. Not that Bear wasn't used to that.

"Sorry." He placed a hand on Mandy's shoulder, drawing the other man's attention to her and visibly putting him a little at ease. "I used to live here. A long time ago."

"A long, long time ago," Mandy added, cracking a smile. She must've noticed the uneasy look on the man's face, too.

"It's a good house." The guy finished walking the box to the back of the truck and placed it in the kid's hands. "But if you're looking for a tour—"

"No, no." Bear gestured to Mandy. "Just wanted to show my kid where I used to hang out. Try to convince her I was cool once."

"It's not working," Mandy added.

Bear ruffled her hair, causing her to shoot daggers in his direction as she smoothed it back down. "Don't want to get in your way. You live here? Or used to?"

"Nah, I'm a couple houses down." He hooked a thumb over his shoulder. "Just helping some friends get through a tough day."

"I know you don't know us, but if you need a couple more pairs of hands—"

"Appreciate it." He did smile now, though it didn't reach his eyes. "We might've taken you up on that about three hours ago, but I think we're almost done now. Thanks, though."

Bear looked back up at the house. "They already have a buyer? Wouldn't mind coming back here every summer. It's a good location."

"They do, yeah." The man looked over his shoulder, and Bear followed his gaze. One of the other men, the father, was staring at them, a concerned look on his face. The man held up a finger and turned back to Bear. "Sorry, gotta get back to work. From what I hear, the management company that bought it will rent this place out. Maybe you'll have a chance to stay here once in a while after all. It was nice meeting you."

"You too," Bear said. Mandy waved politely. "Have a good one."

Bear took one last look at the house before turning Mandy around and heading back in the direction they'd come from. When they were out of earshot, she looked up at him with her eyebrows raised. "Something seems off."

Bear ran a hand down his beard. "You caught that too, huh?"

4

MANDY STOPPED SHORT OF THE ICE CREAM PARLOR AND LOOKED UP AT Bear. "Seriously?"

"What?" He gave her the most innocent face he could muster. "You don't want any ice cream?"

She moved until she blocked his view inside the parlor and placed her hands on her hips. "We both know you're not here for the ice cream."

"I can go home and make us some protein shakes instead."

Mandy walked up to the door and pulled it open. "Oh God. I do not want to sit around all night smelling your protein shake farts." She held her hands out, palms up. "Don't add salt to this wound."

Rosemary's Ice Cream Palace was an oasis, even in the middle of this sandy paradise. Everything had been painted stark white, a soft blush, or pale turquoise. It reminded him of the old-fashioned ice cream parlors his dad used to take him to, but there were enough modern touches to make it feel refreshingly new. In the summer, it'd be full of people—kids, teenagers, parents, grandparents—eating classic flavors or trying Rosie's latest gamble. Even the most deranged combinations somehow turned out well. He suspected she was a witch. But the good kind. Like Glinda. Or Samantha.

In the middle of winter, it was completely dead inside. Not just because of the time of year or the temperatures. There just weren't a lot of people around in general. Bear suspected his business had at least helped keep Rosie afloat over the past couple weeks. And her ice cream had forced him to start working out twice a day.

The doorbell chimed and Rosie called from the back. "Be with you in a minute!"

Mandy stepped up to the counter and made her way through the flavors until she stopped at her usual. Cotton candy. That girl could eat sugar through a tube and think it needed more sugar. Bear preferred something a little savory. A good pecan or salted caramel. But Mandy was nothing if not consistent.

Rosie popped out of the back, wiping her hands on her apron. She was tall and slender, built like a star athlete on a swim team. Her blonde hair was tied back in a low ponytail, and she wore a pair of dark-rimmed glasses. When she saw them, she beamed and the whole parlor seemed to get brighter. "Hey Mandy! Hi Bear."

"Hey Rosie." His voice came out deeper than he'd intended. Mandy shot him a look. He ignored it. "How's it going?"

"I'm really glad you're here, actually." Rosie was slightly out of breath and her southern twang was coming through a little strong. She was either stressed or excited. "One of the syrup lines for the floats is clogged up. I need to flush it, but the nozzle isn't coming off, even with the pliers. Could you give a look at it for me?"

"No problem. Sounds easy enough."

"For you, maybe." She turned to Mandy. "The usual?"

"Yeah." Mandy's voice was flat. She caught Bear's look and stiffened. Cleared her throat. "Thanks."

"You got it." Rosie was already overfilling her biggest paper cup. "What about you, Bear?"

"What's the latest?"

Rosie handed Mandy her ice cream and stepped down to the end of the counter. "Made this one just for you." Bear didn't miss the way she flushed when she said it. "It's a two-scoop combo. You can get them individually, but it won't have the same effect."

"I'm intrigued. Go on."

"First flavor"—She pointed to the bucket in the front—"is coffee ice cream mixed with chocolate espresso swirls and hazelnut toffee. A little bitter, and it'll wake you up. Not recommended as a midnight snack."

Bear chuckled. "Noted."

"The next one," Rosie pointed to the bucket sitting directly behind the first, "is a maple bacon doughnut-flavor. It's got a sweet cream and vanilla base, with maple syrup swirls and chunks of bacon."

Bear steadied her with a look. "What's the secret ingredient? This sounds too normal for you."

"A hint—and I'm talking just a *hint*—of sriracha." Rosie hurried on, her accent peaking again. "There's something so interesting about that sweet-heat combo, especially when you combine it with the bitter coffee. And then you top it all off with a generous helping of rainbow sprinkles, of course."

Bear stared her down for a full ten seconds, enjoying the way she grew increasingly nervous under his gaze, before he broke out in a wide grin. "It sounds incredible. What are you calling this one?"

"Morning Mayhem. You like it?"

"I love it." The laugh that escaped his mouth was genuine. He saw Mandy shake her head out of the corner of his eye. "Let me fix that syrup line, and you can whip me up a bowl." He pulled out his wallet. "How much?"

"No charge. You know that. You help too much as it is. If you won't let me actually pay you with money, then I'll pay you with ice cream."

"Can't turn down a deal like that." He folded a twenty and tucked it into the tip jar, despite her protestations. "For the good company."

They went through this every time he stopped in, and that line made her blush harder every day. "Thanks, Bear. Come on, I'll show you which machine it is."

Bear followed Rosie into the back, feeling Mandy's gaze on the back of his neck the entire time. Then the woman turned on him and lifted an eyebrow without another word. Bear rubbed a hand on the back of his neck. "What?"

"Things getting any better with Mandy?"

Bear huffed out a breath, not quite laughter, not quite a sigh. "Define better?"

"Is she talking back as much?"

"Funny you should say that. I think she's gonna be a comedian. Whole world as her stage. Me as her punchline."

Rosie laid a hand on his shoulder. The warmth of it seeped into his bones. "She loves you. She's just having a tough time right now."

"We've been here for months."

"And she might hate it the entire time you stay. Or she might not."

"Very sound parenting advice." Bear kept a smile on his face. Just teasing. "Thank you." Rosie laughed and took her hand back. The warmth didn't dissipate. He cleared his throat. "Did you really need that nozzle fixed, or—"

"Yes!" She flicked a switch on the side of one machine to turn it off, then pointed toward the nozzle. "This is the one I'm having trouble with."

Bear picked up the wrench from the counter and stepped closer, forcing Rosie to retreat. The back room wasn't that big, and he was aware of how much room he took up. As much as he liked these frequent visits, he hadn't had the courage to ask her out yet. She'd probably say yes. And that was the problem.

Bear clamped the wrench down and twisted it left. It stuck for a second before coming loose. Rosie cheered. Bear felt his chest swell. "Easy peasy."

"You're a life-saver." She turned sheepish. "If I clean one, I might as well clean them all."

"It's no problem."

The chime on the front door rang. "Be there in a second," she called, then turned back to Bear. "Just make sure the machines are off before you undo the nozzle. If you make a mess, you're cleaning it up."

"Yes, ma'am."

Rosie beamed before bouncing back out into the main parlor. Bear didn't hear her customary greeting. Her voice was flat. Apprehensive. "What can I get you today?"

"Large chocolate and vanilla." It was a man's voice. Deep. Gruff. "That's it."

"No sprinkles or chopped nuts? Whipped cream and cherry?"

"I said that's it."

"Got it."

It took Bear less than thirty seconds to flip off all the machines and unhook their nozzles. Then he stepped back out front, leaning against the door jamb to the back. The man turned, and the two of them sized each other up. His hair was shaved closed to his head, but it was obvious he was balding. His nose looked like it'd been broken a few times. Stubble lined a prominent chin.

"Problem out here?" Bear leveled the man with a stern gaze.

"Not your concern."

"Wasn't asking you."

"It's fine, Bear." Rosemary smiled, but Bear could tell she was scared. She handed the man his ice cream. "That'll be ten dollars, please."

"Ten bucks? For this shit?" The man reared his arm back and threw it against the back wall, smearing the chalkboard menu items that Rosie had taken so long to write out in different colors. "No thanks."

Rosie blinked at the mess, like she couldn't quite comprehend what had just happened. Mandy was on her feet now, but one look from Bear, and she took two steps back.

Bear hadn't moved. The man had done it to get a reaction, and Bear wasn't about to give it to him. He forced his voice to stay even. "Hey, what's your name?"

"None of your business." The man matched Bear's tone. "Hey, what's yours?"

"What a coincidence." Bear's smile probably looked manic. "Same as yours."

The man turned to Rosemary and pointed a finger at Bear. "This your new boyfriend? Think he's gonna protect you?"

Bear stood a little straighter. Rosie had known from the beginning that this guy wasn't just a regular customer. Bear had been coming here for weeks, and she'd never mentioned anything to him.

Rosie couldn't look the man in the face. "He's not my boyfriend." Her voice was so small. So scared. "Please. I just need a little more time. There hasn't been a lot of customers. I can't make money if there's no one—"

The man slapped his hand down on the counter, making Rosie and Mandy jump. "Three days. Don't disappoint us."

"Oh, so you're just a goon, huh?" Bear asked. "Who you work for?"

"Funny you should ask that." The man turned his back on Bear and walked toward the door. "Their name is none of your business too."

Bear stalked across the parlor as the man slipped out of the shop. Rosemary ran around the counter and placed a hand on his bicep. He didn't want to stop, but he did. Her eyes were swimming with tears. "Please don't. Don't make it worse."

"I'm just gonna see what direction he's walking in. If he gets into a car."

Rosemary let go, and Bear opened the door after the other man. The chime sounded distant with his blood pumping through his ears and the cold, salty gusts smacking him in the face. But when he made it out to the sidewalk, the guy was nowhere to be found. Maybe he'd slipped between buildings. Or there had already been a car waiting for him with someone else in the driver's seat.

Either way, he was gone.

5

MANDY PUSHED THROUGH THE DOORS OF THE CAPE HATTERAS Secondary School with her shoulders back and her chin held high. She might have hated every second of every minute of every day that she spent in this hellhole, but she wouldn't let anyone know that. No weaknesses. That was her motto.

That was hard when everyone stared at her.

Bear had taught her about the importance of going unnoticed. Sticking to the shadows. It was hard to do that in a school with fewer than four hundred students. Mandy was the new girl. Worse, she would forever be the new girl. Not a lot of people moved to the Outer Banks these days. All these kids had been born and raised here, just like their parents and grandparents before them. Most of these kids had grown up together. Everyone knew everyone. Their mothers were best friends —or, at least, best frenemies—who took girls' trips together. Their dads hung out to watch football every Sunday.

Everyone else only visited the coast for the summer. They didn't make a habit out of wintering here. And lately, even those numbers were shrinking. Bear thought it was weird, though he didn't say it out loud. He thought she didn't pay attention, but she did.

Her only hope was that they wouldn't be here forever. Something would happen, and they'd move on to the next town. To a new school. And she'd be the new girl all over again. She didn't look forward to that, but maybe they'd end up in a place where it was easier to avoid the spotlight.

The hallway was crowded with kids at this point in the morning. The first bell would ring in a minute or two. Everyone stood at their lockers, putting their coats away and picking up what books they'd need to their first period. Gossiping and checking their phones one last time. They were all so boring. So regular. Part of her wished they could know the things she'd seen and done. Part of her liked that it was her little secret. Something she could hold over their heads.

Dottie MacDonald stepped away from her group of friends and stopped in front of Mandy. She was tall for her age, with stick-straight hair so blonde it almost looked white. She had perfect bangs held back by a little black headband. She insisted on dressing in little blazers and skirts every day, like she was preparing herself for becoming president of the United States. No one thought she was nerdy or uncool. Everyone wanted to be her friend.

Everyone except Mandy.

"Good morning," Dottie said, loud enough for half the hallway to hear. Several students turned in their direction. "You know, there's no shame in asking for help, Mandy. You don't have to wear the same sweatshirt to school every day. I'd let you borrow one of mine, but I don't think it'd fit."

"Yeah, I don't think it would either. Definitely too big."

Mandy waited to see the look of shock and annoyance on the other girl's face before she brushed past her down the hall, toward her own locker. Dottie's barbs were getting weaker, and Mandy found they didn't bother her as much. When Mandy had first gotten here, the girl had tried to become friends with her, but Mandy could see right through it. Now everyone knew Dottie hated the new girl. So no one else would be friends with her either.

The first bell rang out just as Mandy shut her locker and turned on her heel toward her homeroom. She filed in behind the other students and made her way to the back of the classroom, picking the seat in the corner, right next to the windows. As soon as she sat and thunked her backpack to the ground, the girl in front of her turned around.

Jenny Pickett was the only other girl in school almost as weird as Mandy. The funny thing was, she didn't look all that different from Dottie. Her blonde hair was a shade darker, but just as straight and long. She wore it in a ponytail, chewing on its ends when she was concentrating on something interesting or difficult. Jenny didn't wear skirts, but she did wear blazers and dark glasses that magnified her blue eyes to almost comical proportions.

If Dottie was smart, then Jenny was a genius. Probably another reason why Dottie had turned the whole school against the other girl— she didn't like being outshined. Not that Jenny cared. She didn't go out of her way to make friends.

If Mandy was being honest, sometimes she felt bad for Jenny. The kids at school weren't nice, and as much as Jenny pretended not to hear what they were saying, it was hard to ignore. That's how they'd first become friends—Mandy stopped a ninth-grade girl from pushing her around, and Jenny had muttered an appreciative thanks. After that, Mandy had asked if they could sit together at lunch, and the other girl had agreed. No one ever bothered them, and over the next couple months, Jenny had opened up to her more and more.

Mandy tried to convince herself it was just tactical. School wasn't always easy for her, and Jenny was the smartest girl in their grade. She'd also grown up here, so she knew who everyone was and what their parents did for a living and whose mother had gotten caught sleeping with whose father. Jenny Pickett was a goldmine of information, and Mandy would be stupid not to tap into that.

Though it wasn't just that. Jenny was also nice. She never acted like she thought Mandy belonged in an institution. Maybe Mandy wouldn't be able to tell Jenny everything about herself, but she could trust her enough to tell her some. For now, that was enough.

"Do you want to go to the beach tonight and look for coins?" Jenny asked.

"You know my dad won't let me do that." Bear was his usual overprotective self. Even here in a dead town where everyone knew everyone, he saw dangers around every corner. "If I'm not home right after school, he starts to panic."

"We could always stop at your house first so he doesn't worry." Jenny's voice was light and high. She sounded as innocent as she looked. Even that wouldn't be good enough for Bear.

"It's not going to work." Plus, Mandy was nervous about Jenny meeting her dad. What if the other girl thought differently of her after that? "We could always skip tomorrow. He'd never know."

Jenny squirmed in her chair. "Not come to school at all?"

"We'd have more daylight hours to look for coins and less chance for someone's parents to spot us since they're all at work."

"Did you know that in 1585, the Queen ordered some of her explorers to setup a military base in the Outer Banks for the sole purpose of robbing Spanish ships?"

Mandy smiled. Jenny liked to tell her fun facts about pirates when she was nervous. "No, I didn't."

"It's true. And they weren't called pirates when they had orders from the Queen like that. They were called privateers."

"That's interesting." Mandy thought back on some of the other information Jenny had shared with her over the last couple of months. "Maybe we'll be able to find some coins that once belonged to Blackbeard."

"Blackbeard was mostly on Ocracoke."

"Yeah, but that stuff moves around all the time, right? And just because there's less evidence of him being here doesn't mean he wasn't, you know?"

Jenny chewed her lip. "That's true."

"If we get caught skipping, I'll tell everyone it was my idea and I talked you into it."

"It was your idea," Jenny pointed out. "And you did talk me into it."

Mandy grinned. "So, that's a yes?"

Jenny didn't need to answer. The light in her eyes was enough. "There was this couple who spent decades collecting coins from the beach. Some of them dated back thousands of years. I'd like to find one of those."

"Maybe we will." Mandy watched as their teacher entered the classroom. Some of the kids stopped talking to their friends, but there was still a general murmur among the class. Mandy leaned forward. "Do you have a metal detector?"

"Not allowed to have them on the beaches." Jenny didn't look disappointed. "Have to do it by hand."

"Good thing we have all day, then," Mandy muttered. The teacher started calling names, but Mandy had one more thing on her mind. "Hey, you ever hang out at the Ice Cream Palace?"

"Yeah! I love Rosemary's cotton candy ice cream."

"I knew we were friends for a reason." Jenny beamed at this, and Mandy continued on. "Anything weird ever happen there?"

"Weird like what?"

"I don't know, just weird." Mandy didn't want to give too much away. "Do you think Rosemary's hiding anything?"

"I doubt it. She's so nice. She always gives me extra cherries. Why would she have to hide anything?"

Mandy thought back on the strange man who'd thrown the ice cream against the wall. Bear had been in the back, but Mandy had seen the way the woman had looked at him when he'd first walked in. Like she knew exactly why he was there.

Mandy just shrugged and sat back in her seat. Under her breath, she muttered, "That's what I'm trying to figure out."

6

BEFORE BEAR COULD RAISE HIS FIST TO KNOCK ON THE MURRAYS' FRONT door, Muriel opened it and grinned at him. "Morning Bear."

"Morning Mrs. Murray." Bear gave her a scrutinizing look. "How'd you know it was me?"

"You're always on time." She stepped to the side and held out her hand. "Come on in."

Bear walked through the door, shutting it behind him and taking a deep breath. It smelled like freshly baked cookies. His mouth watered, and he was transported back to his grandmother's house. Muriel's chocolate chip cookies tasted exactly the same, like they'd been working off the same recipe.

"Made your favorite," she said, noticing the dreamy looking on his face. "You can have one before you get started, if you'd like."

"Would be rude to say no," Bear said.

Muriel laughed and waved him toward the kitchen. She moved slowly, shuffling her feet and trailing one hand along the wall in case she stumbled. Both the Murrays were in good health, but one little accident could change all of that.

Joseph sat at the dining room table reading the paper. He looked up and pointed to the flickering light overhead. "See what I mean?"

Bear held up his toolkit. "Probably just old wiring. Shouldn't take too much to fix it. I'll be in and out."

"You know you can stay as long as you want." Muriel held a plate of cookies out to him. "We enjoy your company."

"I appreciate that." Bear set his toolbox down and took a cookie. "I've got the whole afternoon free if you need anything else."

Joseph folded the paper and placed it on the table, then stared over the top of his spectacles. "And what about young Rosie? Is she busy this afternoon?"

Bear shook his head with a laugh. "I didn't ask."

"Maybe you should, son. Before someone else does."

"You leave him alone, Joseph Arthur Murray." Muriel set the plate of cookies back down on the counter and put her hands on her hips. "You have the subtlety of a wrecking ball, dear."

Joseph shrugged. "I seem to recall it working out in my favor, don't you?"

Muriel waved him off with a playful shake of her head. "Rosemary's not going anywhere. She'd be silly to with a man like Bear knocking on her door."

"I'm not knocking on anyone's door." Bear slipped another cookie from the plate.

"Metaphorically speaking." Muriel's grin widened. "Did you go see her yesterday?"

Memories of the man at the ice cream parlor made Bear frown. Rosie had clammed up the second he'd started to ask questions, saying that some people were mad she'd had to raise her prices.

"Bear?" Muriel shook him from his thoughts. "Everything okay?"

"Yeah, yeah." When both the Murrays leveled him with a look, he shrugged. "Someone came in the shop yesterday. Hair shaved close to his head. A little shorter than me. Big chin. Aggressive. He ordered ice cream, then threw it against the wall."

Muriel gasped. "Oh dear. Is Rosie okay? Did anything happen?"

"Nothing happened, but she didn't want to talk about it. You ever see someone like that around here?"

Muriel and Joseph exchanged a look. Joseph spoke first. "Doesn't sound familiar, but we don't get out much."

"You sure Rosie's okay?"

"I'll check on her later today." Bear wagged his finger at the older woman. "But just to check on her. I won't go knocking on her door."

Muriel shrugged. "Your loss, dear."

Don't I know it. "First thing's first." Bear shoved the rest of his cookie in his mouth, then turned to his toolbox. "Let's see what we're dealing with here."

Joseph and Muriel retreated to the living room, allowing Bear space to work on the chandelier over the dining room table. It was silver with dozens of crystals hanging off each arm and not a speck of dust on them. Removing it was the most difficult part of the job. Something told him it was antique, and totally irreplaceable.

Fixing the faulty wiring proved much easier. It only took about fifteen minutes, and he already had everything he needed. At this rate, he'd have time to help them with a couple more projects around the house before he went to check on Rosie.

Bear didn't think much of it when the doorbell rang. He was too busy wondering what else he could tackle today. The Murrays lived modestly, but they'd created a beautiful home. It was strange to think they'd been here in the eighties when he'd been a kid, and well before that. Had he ever passed them on the street? Ran by them on the beach? Egged their house? He'd been a menace as a kid, but at least he made up for it now.

Joseph's voice carried through the house from the front door and gave Bear pause. "I told you, we're not interested." There was a muffled response before the old man spoke again. "Some people care about more than money." Another muffled response. "I know what you're doing, and it's not going to work."

That's when Bear set down his tools and walked toward the front of the house. Muriel stood behind her husband, her hands clasped in front of her. A man stood on the porch in front of them, one hand on the door, preventing Joseph from closing it on him.

"There a problem out here?" Bear asked, coming up behind the Murrays, feeling like a giant amongst dwarves.

The man on the porch looked up at him in surprise, immediately taking his hand off the door. He wore a navy-blue suit with pinstripes and carried a leather briefcase that looked like it'd cost half the Murrays' social security check. "Hello sir. I didn't realize anyone else was home."

"Clearly." Bear has seen people like this before, taking advantage of the elderly. Either through manipulation or physical strength. Bear was a lot harder to push around. "Otherwise, you wouldn't be harassing these fine people."

The man laughed. "How is it harassment if I'm offering them money?"

"Because he told you no. You should leave. Before you get hurt."

"Is that a threat?" The man's facade twisted into a predator's sneer. "It's not a good idea to threaten me."

Bear opened his mouth to retort, but Muriel laid a frail hand on his arm. She looked back at the man and said, "It wasn't a threat. But you should leave now."

A salesman's smile spread across his face again. "Think about my offer." His gaze shifted to Bear. "Have a good day."

Joseph closed the door after him and locked it, throwing the deadbolt with a sigh. He and Muriel exchanged a look, both of their lips tight and thin. They refused to meet Bear's eyes.

"Anyone gonna fill me in?"

Joseph waved him off, shuffling back over to his recliner. "Someone looking to buy the house. Won't take no for an answer."

"Do you know who he is? Who he represents? We could file a complaint."

Joseph sank into his chair with a groan. "Not worth it."

"Maybe we should consider it," Muriel said. "We are getting older—"

"He's offering us half the house's worth." Joseph's tone bit Bear to his core. "The market is good right now. We could get a lot more money if we hired our own agent."

"The Kramers couldn't sell their house." Muriel's voice was tight with worry. "They ended up getting a lot less than their initial offer."

"What's the company name?" Bear pressed. "Let me look into this."

"No." Joseph wouldn't look at Bear. "No point in causing more trouble for ourselves."

"If you're in some sort of trouble—"

"No." Joseph looked up. A stubbornness in his eyes told Bear no amount of pushing or prodding would get him to open up. "Let us know when you're done with that light, and Muriel will send you home with some lasagna."

Bear took that as his cue to clean up his tools and head out.

7

Less than an hour later, a freshly showered Bear pulled open the door to Rosemary's Ice Cream Palace, greeted by its customary chime. This time, Rosie sat behind the counter reading a book. She looked up when Bear entered and smiled, a tinge of yesterday's fear lingering around the edges.

She set her book down. "You're early."

"That okay?" Bear was suddenly nervous. Unsure.

"Of course." Rosie bit her lip and closed her book. "I'm sorry about yesterday."

"You have nothing to apologize for. You didn't do anything wrong."

"I know." She didn't sound like she meant it. "But that was embarrassing."

"You ready to tell me what's going on yet?"

Rosie sighed and stood, putting her elbows on the counter in front of her, stretching her muscles as she did so. "At the end of last summer, we had a lot of vandalism. It started off small. Graffiti, that sort of thing. It was annoying, but nothing we couldn't handle."

"We?"

"Wasn't just me." She stood up straight and popped her back, a look of relief flooding her face. "All the businesses up and down this street.

And a couple the next one over. Some of it was fine, just names and designs. Others were a little more graphic. Considering how many kids are around, that wasn't going to fly."

"You said it started off small," Bear prompted.

She nodded. "We'd clean it off, cover it up, do the best we could. It always came back. A few of the shops that could afford it put up cameras to try to catch them in the act. We could never figure it out, though. And as soon as the cameras went up, things escalated."

"How?"

"Broken windows. Broken locks." She gestured to the counter in front of her. "Someone broke in and stole money from my register. I started taking my cash home every night after that. They also messed with a couple of my machines, and I had to get them fixed."

"And you never figured out who it was?" Bear asked.

"Nope." She shrugged, almost like it didn't matter. "A week later, some guy showed up, told me he'd make sure no one messed with my shop if I slipped him some money. I refused at first. Things got a lot worse. Some of the other shopkeepers told me they started paying and everything went back to normal."

"So you started paying too." There was no accusation in Bear's voice.

Rosie shrugged again. "I felt like I didn't have a choice."

"What are the chances the guys collecting the money were the same guys destroying property?"

"Pretty high." Rosie crossed her arms over her chest. The effect made her look even smaller than usual. "I'm not dumb. I knew what was going on. But I couldn't afford to keep replacing my machines."

"Was that the same guy who came in yesterday?"

She shook her head. "They switch out every couple weeks. Probably so we can't figure out who they are. That guy yesterday has only been around a week or two." Rosie swallowed and looked up at Bear. "He scares me."

Bear took a step closer. He wanted to reach out to her, to hug her, to comfort her, but something made him stop. He reached into his wallet and pulled out a wad of cash, holding it out to her. "Take this."

"Bear, no." She was staring down at the money like it was the solution to all her problems. "I can't do that. It's not fair."

"It's a gift." He took another couple of steps forward and gently placed it on the counter. "Just so you can catch up. In case we don't figure out a better solution."

Rosie finally met his eyes. "Are you sure?"

"I'm sure." He made certain his voice didn't hold any doubt. "You don't know who this guy works for?"

Rosie shook her head, then slipped the money into the front pocket of her jeans. "No one else does, either. I think everyone's too afraid to ask. Rob down at the souvenir shop refused to pay. He ended up in a bad car accident two days later. I don't think it was a coincidence."

Bear's jaw clenched. "When he comes to collect in a couple days, give him the money. Act normal. I'll be outside, around back. I'll figure out who he is, and where he's going."

"Bear, I—"

Bear reached across the counter and put a hand on Rosie's shoulder. "I'm good at this. Trust me, okay? I just want to know who he's working for. Maybe we can figure out a better long-term solution without you depleting your savings."

Rosie's laugh was bitter. "Too late for that." Then she tipped her head back. "God, I could use a drink."

"Place is empty," Bear said. "Why don't you close up early? I'm buying."

"Bear, you just handed me a couple hundred dollars. I can't—"

"I'm going with or without you," Bear said, his voice light as he took a step toward the door. "But I could really use the company."

After only a second's more hesitation, she grabbed her keys, flipped the sign on the door, and locked the shop. Bear had the urge to take her hand as they headed toward Teach's Tavern, a cheesy Blackbeard-themed bar that had the best drinks on the island. The locals hated that they loved it, and Bear found himself in solid agreement with them. But there would be beer. And Rosemary. That's all that mattered.

Twenty minutes later, the pair were perched on stools at one end of the bar, a bottle of Weeping Radish Corolla Gold lager in each of their hands. Bear had just told some stupid joke, and Rosie had her head thrown back in laughter. A few heads turned in their direction, and Bear couldn't help the way his chest swelled in response. Everyone knew and loved Rosemary, and he'd been the one to make that sound come out of her mouth. He took another swig of his beer to keep his thoughts from spilling out.

Rosie set her bottle down on the bar and looked at him with an eyebrow raised. Then she shook her head and glanced away, another small laugh escaping.

"What?" Bear said. "Was the joke that bad?"

"Yes." She looked back. "But no, that's not it. You're just, I dunno, a good person, Bear. Like, a really good person."

"You sound shocked."

"I'm not. I knew from the moment you walked into my shop that you'd be the good kind of trouble."

He liked the sound of that. "Thanks, I think."

"You're welcome." Her gaze drifted and a peaceful silence passed between them. She looked like she wanted to say something else. Instead, she slapped her hands down on the bar and slid from her stool. "I have to pee!"

Bear chuckled as he watched her head toward the bathroom, then turned back to scan the rest of the bar. Besides grabbing a drink and spending time with Rosie, Bear had a third point of business here. He wanted to know if Big Chin himself hung out at the local pub, or if anyone else who looked like him would be in attendance.

There were maybe a dozen or so patrons in the bar. Bear knew most of them by sight if not by name. This wasn't his first stop at Teach's, and he recognized a couple regulars. The ones he didn't recognize looked like vacationers. Young couples who came to the Outer Banks in the winter because it was cheaper. They mostly kept to themselves.

Rosie returned a moment later, that silly grin still on her face. Bear ordered them another round. As soon as the bartender set the bottles in front of them, a pair of men walked through the front door, stopping to scan the miniscule crowd. The one in front was about as tall as Bear with an extra fifty pounds on him. He had an unkempt beard that reached the center of his chest and wore a pair of sunglasses on his head. His friend behind him was shorter and leaner, his face cleanshaven. Bear didn't recognize either of them.

Rosie turned to see what Bear was staring at, then whipped back around, ducking her head. "Shit. Did he see me?"

Bear looked back at the men and noticed the cleanshaven one heading in their direction. "Afraid so. Who are they?"

"Trouble." Rosie looked up at Bear. "An ex."

Bear lifted his beer to his lips and watched as the bigger one stopped halfway down the bar to order drinks. The smaller one kept walking toward them, taking in Bear and then switching his gaze over to Rosie.

"Hey Rosie," he said. His voice was higher than Bear expected. "Nice seeing you here."

"Hey Jed." Rosie turned toward him with a pained grin on her face. "How're you?"

"Tried to get ahold of you a couple times." He let the words hang in the air.

"Yeah. Been busy."

"You're not busy now. Come have a drink with us."

Bear chuckled. "Take a hint, man. Desperation doesn't look good on you."

Jed finally made eye contact with Bear. "And who are you?"

"A friend," Bear answered. "Who are you?"

Jed leaned forward and ran one finger down Rosemary's arm. "We knocked boots back in the day."

Bear shrugged and took another sip of his drink. "To err is human."

Rosie's eyes widened. She tried and failed to hold back her laugh, attempting to cover it up with a cough instead. "I'm busy, Jed. I don't want to have drinks with you. We ended a long time ago. Let's leave it in the past."

Jed's eyes went dark. "Him? Really? What's he have that I don't?"

"Six inches—take that however you want. A hairline. And the ability to grow a beard."

Jed lurched forward, knocking over Rosemary's beer and forcing her off the stool. Bear kept his eye on her but didn't move. The bearded wonder at the end of the bar walked over to the group. "Problem here?"

"Not yet," Bear said, before Jed could answer. "But there will be if you can't control your friend."

"Our new friend is a smartass, Roy. I'm not sure I appreciate that."

Bear took another swig of his beer, then set it out of the way before standing. "Fellas, I'll be honest with you, I'm looking to let off a little steam. No matter how it ends, it won't be in your favor. Walk away."

Jed took a step toward Bear like he was looking to test that theory, but between one blink and the next, Rosie moved in between them, pushing Jed back. Bear had seen the way she tossed around those buckets of ice cream. She was stronger than she looked. Jed stumbled back a step or two, never taking his eyes off Bear.

"Go away, Jed. It's over. It's been over. I'm not interested. Try to talk to me one more time, and I'll get a restraining order. Move on."

Jed looked hurt and angry and like he wanted to prove a point, but the whole bar was watching now. A few people were standing, waiting to see if they needed to intervene. Bear hadn't been lying about needing to blow off some steam, and it took every ounce of his willpower not to egg the other men on. He didn't want to be the bad guy here.

Jed shook his head, turning his back on Bear. "Come on, Roy. She's not worth it."

Bear watched as the two of them grabbed their beers from the bartender and went outside to sit on the back patio. Rosie turned back to him with her eyebrows raised again. "What?" he asked, innocently.

"Maybe I was wrong about you being good trouble." Her tone was still light, but she hadn't sat down yet.

Bear shrugged. "He started it."

"Is it bad I was kind of hoping you'd finish it?"

Bear had to fight back a grin. "You would've felt guilty tomorrow."

"Maybe." Her eyes sparkled in the neon signs above the bar. "Come on, walk me home. I don't want those bozos jumping out of a bush at me."

Bear was all too happy to comply.

8

BEAR'S HIGH FROM WALKING ROSEMARY HOME AND RECEIVING A
lingering 'thank you' hug deflated as soon as he walked through his
front door. Mandy stood at the door, hands on her hips, like an angry
wife after her husband was late for dinner. But it wasn't even five yet.

"Where have you been?" she asked.

"Went to check on Rosemary."

Mandy stepped closer and sniffed the air. "You checked on her over
drinks?"

He peered down at her, caught somewhere between exasperation
and laughter. Mandy was rocket fuel in a small human body. It was one
of the things he loved about her—one of the things that would keep her
safe later on. It also drove him crazy. She was a thirty-five-year-old
woman trapped inside a teenage body.

"She had a rough day at the parlor. No one was there. I invited her
out to get her mind off everything."

"I was worried, you know." Mandy's voice was still tough, but he saw
the truth of it in her eyes. "When you weren't here."

Bear stepped up to her and kissed the top of her head. "I'm sorry. I
should've left a note. I went next door to fix their light, and they got it

into my head that I should check on Rose after yesterday. I wasn't thinking straight."

"Clearly." Mandy gave him a significant look, but she was back to blustering now. "How come you're allowed to leave, and I'm not?"

"Because you're a child, and I'm an adult."

Mandy waved that away. "Besides the point. Maybe I had somewhere to be! Something to do!"

"The only thing you should be doing after school is your homework."

"It's done, if you must know." She glanced down toward the floor. "Mostly. I have to call Jenny later for help with math." She smirked up at him. "Unless you want to help?"

Bear raised his hands in surrender. "I think Jenny is the expert here."

"Speaking of somewhere to be." Mandy was getting less subtle with her changes in topic. "Can I go to the beach with Jenny?"

"It's getting dark."

"Come on, Bear. Please?"

"No." Bear left no room for discussion. "It's not safe."

"What's the point in training me to take care of myself if you still keep me locked up in an ivory tower?"

"You know we can't afford an ivory tower." Bear walked into the kitchen and popped open the refrigerator. "It's made out of bricks. You should be grateful. Some kids have to live in wooden towers. Think of the splinters."

"You know what I'm trying to say." Mandy huffed as she sat down in a kitchen chair. "Jenny's been telling me all this cool stuff about pirates and the things you can find on the beach. There are coins that could be worth thousands of dollars!"

Bear hummed his agreement, half listening to what she was saying. He was barely registering the contents of the fridge now. Images of Jed and Roy lurking in the shadows took over. Would Jed try to go after Rosemary when Bear wasn't around? Bear had told her to lock up tight and not leave for the rest of the night. But what if the men showed up on his doorstep? He wasn't worried about being able to handle the pair of them, but what about Mandy? She might not be able to get away.

"Anyone approaches you on the street." Bear cut her off mid-sentence. Something about shipwrecks and Blackbeard. "You run in the other direction, you got it? Don't try to be tough."

"Are you even listening to what I'm saying?" Mandy groaned. "Seriously? Did you hear anything?"

"And not just the man from the shop." Bear twisted to look at her over his shoulder. "Anyone try to talk to you, you run."

Mandy's eyes narrowed. "What happened?"

"Nothing happened."

"What *almost* happened?"

The fridge started beeping, so Bear shut the door and leaned back against the countertop. "Rosemary's ex. Man named Jed. And his friend Roy. Didn't want to take no for an answer."

"Typical." Mandy rolled her eyes. She was trying to sound uninterested, but Bear knew better. "You fight them?"

"No, but it might've been better if I had."

"Then they would've gotten their asses kicked and known better?"

"Exactly." He sighed. "Something weird is going on around here."

"Something weird is always going on." Mandy threw up her hands in exasperation. "No matter where we go or what we do, there's always something."

"I thought you said this place was boring."

"It *is* boring, but do you remember the last place we lived? Giant pharmaceutical company covering up illegal testing of drugs as a bioweapon. Don't exactly want to relive that."

"Well, there's no pharmaceutical company around here, so—"

"*You know what I mean.*" There was real fire in Mandy's eyes now. "Seriously, Bear, is this all going to blow up in our faces again? Because if so, I'd rather leave before it does."

"We're not leaving."

"So it *is* going to blow up in our faces?"

"Let's take it one day at a time." Bear wished he could reassure Mandy, but he didn't want to lie to her. Truth was, he had no idea how this was going to play out. He had no idea what was going on. "I'm serious, though. Keep your eyes open. I'm counting on you. Don't go wandering off. Jenny's house and back, that's all you're allowed, okay?"

Mandy rolled her eyes so hard, Bear though they'd get stuck up there. "Fine. Guess I won't be having any fun ever again in my whole life."

"Nope. Never. I'm the fun police. Here to protect and serve you the most mundane life imaginable."

"I don't think that's how that saying goes," Mandy said.

Bear had a retort on the tip of his tongue. A loud screech from the road out front cut him off. The most excruciating sound Bear had ever heard in his life followed.

9

"IT's NOT THAT BAD," MANDY SAID. "JUST BECAUSE IT's NOT *YOUR* MUSIC doesn't mean it's not good."

"Yes, it does." Bear screwed up his face. "You can't even understand the lyrics. What's the point?"

"You're supposed to *feel* the music," Mandy said. "You don't always need lyrics. Think of classical music."

"I'd rather not."

The sound ratcheted higher. Bear and Mandy turned toward the front of the house in unison. He had expected the noise to move on after a minute. Probably just some teenager thinking he was cool, annoying the neighbors as he passed through. But it didn't dissipate. It kept getting louder.

Mandy winced like the noise caused her physical pain now. She had to shout over the music for Bear to hear her. "It sounds like they parked right on our front porch."

"Wait here," Bear said. When Mandy shook her head and pointed to her ears, he held up a finger. Whatever was going on, he didn't want her involved.

The likelihood that this was just some kid wanting to piss off his neighbors was high, but on the off chance it was something else, Bear didn't want to take his chances.

He stopped short of opening the blinds to look out the window. Since when had he started thinking of Rosie as part of their family? The events of the last day had linked them together. Whoever had hassled her at the shop thought they were dating, and that could be enough reason to send her a warning. He'd fully expected to get a warning of his own.

Looking over his shoulder at Mandy, who was still sitting at the kitchen table, Bear wondered if he should warn her again to stay sharp. She had received his earlier message loud and clear, but she still had a habit of doing what she wanted. She could usually get out of any scrap she found herself in, but one of these days, that might not be true. He hoped he was long dead before that happened.

He turned his attention back to the window and parted the blinds with his thumb and forefinger. The porch was clear, as was the road in front. The music was so loud that the bass rattled the glass window-panes. Another couple decibels, and he wouldn't be surprised if they shattered completely.

Panning his gaze to the left, he noticed only one car parked along the street. Its headlights were switched off and the interior remained empty. He panned his gaze to the right and found the culprit. A black Ford Explorer. It looked brand new. Probably had a state-of-the-art sound system. Maybe custom-built.

Bear stalked over to the window to the right of the door. The one that viewed the Murrays' driveway, right where the Explorer was parked. Bear had a better view of it now and could see the driver, leaning against the hood of the car smoking a cigarette like he had no care in the world.

It was the man from the ice cream shop.

He was parked at the end of the Murrays' driveway, blocking in Joseph's little blue Honda, staring at the house with a shit-eating grin on his face. He bobbed his head to the music, but there was no way he could pick out anything from the noise, other than the bassline.

What was he doing outside the Murrays'? Did he think that's where Bear lived? Was this the warning he'd been expecting, but the man had gotten the address wrong? The guy he'd met in the shop hadn't seemed stupid. Sure, he was working for someone else, but Bear had seen this kind of criminal before. Shrewd and calculated. Sadistic. He wouldn't mess up something as important as an address. Not when he was trying to drive his point home.

Before Bear could decide whether to leave the relative safety of his house, Joseph Murray opened his front door and shouted something from his porch. The man at the end of the driveway waved at him cheerfully.

Joseph shook a finger at the man, but his words were drowned out by the noise. His only option was to descend the steps and get closer to the perpetrator, despite wearing slippers and a housecoat. Bear remembered how big the baldheaded man was, and next to Joseph, he looked like a giant.

Despite that, Joseph poked a finger into the man's chest, shouting something else Bear couldn't hear. He wasn't sure if the baldheaded man heard it, but one minute Joseph had been toe to toe with the guy, and the next he was sprawled across the sidewalk, writhing in agony.

Bear didn't have to think.

Yanking open his front door, he ignored the steps down to the ground and landed with a thud on a patch of grass in his own yard. It only took three giant steps before he was standing at the end of the Murrays' driveway. The baldheaded man had a split second to register Bear's presence before a fist landed against his cheekbone. The man stumbled and tripped over his own feet, falling first against his vehicle, then sliding to the ground.

Bear took the few extra seconds to reach inside the open window of the Explorer and turn the music off. As his hand wrapped about the keys, the other man's fist connected with Bear's stomach, sending him back a step. He didn't go down. And at least it was quiet now.

Baldy sneered. "I can get you on assault for that."

Bear caught movement out of the corner of his eye. Muriel was on the porch, her hands to her mouth. She looked terrified, but she started down the steps. Bear held up his hand. "Stay up there."

The woman didn't argue.

Bear turned his attention back to the older man groaning in pain. He knelt down beside Joseph, keeping Baldy in his periphery. "You okay? Anything broken?"

"Don't think so." Joseph groaned again. "Gonna have a helluva bruise."

"Can you get up on your own?"

"I-I don't think so."

Baldy took a step closer. "You hear what I said?"

Bear ignored him. He had three options. If he left Joseph where he was, the other man would sustain more injuries. If he helped Joseph up the stairs himself, there was a good chance Baldy would attack him from behind. That left option three. He needed help.

Muriel wasn't in any condition to lift her husband, and Bear didn't want her any closer than she already was. That left one other person. If Baldy hadn't already seen her at the ice cream shop, Bear wouldn't risk putting her on his radar.

Bear turned toward the house, keeping his eye on Baldy. "Mandy!" Mandy opened the door in less than three seconds. She had left the security of the kitchen to spy. Bear decided to let that go. He needed her now. "Come over here. Help Mr. Murray inside."

Mandy didn't hesitate. She hopped off the porch and ran over, giving Baldy a wide berth. Then she looped one of Joseph's arms over her shoulders and gently helped the man stand. Once she had him secure, Bear gave Baldy his full attention.

Baldy looked like he was trying to pass a kidney stone. "I said, I can get you—"

"You tripped is all. Hit your face on the side of your fancy car. You really should be more careful. I've got three witnesses." Bear looked around, left to right and back again. "Do you have any witnesses?"

"I let you off easy back at the shop. Didn't want to embarrass you in front of your girlfriend. But she's not here right now, is she?"

"Listen, pal." Bear shifted his stance a little wider. Tensed his stomach muscles. He refused to throw the first punch, but he wouldn't take it lying down. "I don't want to fight you."

"You should be scared."

Bear huffed out a laugh. "No, really. I don't want to fight you. It's not going to end well for you. Maybe I'll get my kid back out here." He'd never do it, but the empty threat was worth seeing the way the man's eyes bugged out of his head. "Still wouldn't be a fair fight, but you'd have a little bit better chance."

Baldy ground his teeth together. He was smart enough to not keep talking, but still dumb enough to charge Bear. At the last second, Bear stepped to the side and grabbed Baldy by the back of the shirt, throwing him forward and using his own momentum against him. Baldy went down hard, getting a face full of dirt and grass and sliding until he hit the sidewalk in front of the Murrays' house.

If Joseph had been left lying there, he would've sustained more injuries.

Baldy growled and looked up at Bear. He'd skinned the top of his head along the concrete, and it was already bleeding. The man had gotten off easy as far as Bear was concerned.

"Leave," Bear said with no bravado in his voice. No fear. No excitement. He was bored of the situation. "Now."

Baldy stood and took his time brushing himself off, wiping as much of the dirt and grass from his clothes as he could. He put his fingers to his head, then scowled when they came back bloody. Then he looked back up at Bear with fire in his eyes. "You're going to pay for that."

"Put it on my tab." Bear stepped to the side and gestured to the vehicle behind him. "It's time for you to go."

Baldy stalked toward him. For a minute Bear thought that was the end of it. Just as the other man passed by him, he threw a jab at Bear's head. It wouldn't have done a lot of damage, but it would've been enough to knock him off balance if Bear hadn't seen it coming.

He grabbed Baldy's fist before it connected and twisted his arm behind his back, shoving him forward and forcing him face-first into the side of the Explorer. The man went down like a bag of bricks.

Bear sighed. A little smear of blood marred the side of the car. The man had crumbled, his wallet falling out of his side pocket. Bear stepped close enough to grab it and look at the license before opening the driver's side door and none too gently shoving the man inside. A second later, his new friend was blinking up at him as Bear held the wallet over his head.

"Mr. Andrew Doyle. It's nice to meet you." Bear tossed the wallet into the man's lap. "You have sixty seconds to get your shit together and leave. Might want to check out that head wound. It looks serious."

His new friend Doyle had enough wherewithal to pull his legs inside the car before Bear slammed the door shut. The man didn't even bother buckling his seatbelt before he took off down the road, swerving slightly and nearly clipping another car parked across the street.

As soon as the Explorer was out of sight, Bear jogged up to the Murrays' front porch, then straight through the open door to the living room. Mandy had deposited Joseph into his recliner and now stood to his left while Muriel hovered to his right.

The older woman looked up when Bear walked inside. "Is he gone?"

"For now." He looked at Joseph. "You doing okay?"

"As good as can be." He winced. "Thank you."

"Want to tell me what that was about?"

Muriel tucked a blanket around her husband's shoulders. "They didn't like that we said no yesterday. I told you things were just going to get worse. Why did you have to go out there and aggravate him, Joseph? He would've gone away eventually. He could've killed you!"

Joseph glared at her until she caught his expression and shut her mouth. He turned back to Bear. "Sorry to bring trouble to your doorstep. Thank you."

"He have something to do with the suit who showed up yesterday?" Bear scratched at his beard. "What aren't you telling me?"

"It's fine, Bear." Joseph's voice left no room for discussion. "We'll be okay."

Bear knew when to push and when to give someone space. Right now, Joseph's pride and ego were bruised as much as his ribcage. Bear would try again tomorrow. Maybe he'd be able to get something out of Muriel. "Call me if you need anything."

The Murrays nodded in silent agreement. Bear took Mandy by the hand, and together, they headed back home. There was nothing else to do tonight.

10

THE SUN WAS BRIGHT IN THE SKY AS MANDY WATCHED THE SCHOOL BUS drive away from her hiding spot behind a tree. She couldn't stop the giggle that escaped her mouth. She'd executed the first part of her plan perfectly. Bear had left early to do something he didn't want to tell her about, so she didn't have to worry about him seeing her playing hooky for the day.

He probably would've murdered her.

She didn't want to think about what would happen if she got caught. Bear was protective on a normal day, but after Rosie and Joseph getting pushed around? He'd be on high alert.

She could also bank on him being distracted.

Mandy turned on her heel and walked in the opposite direction of the bus. Jenny lived a few blocks down and over. It would've been easier if she'd had a bike. Especially because she had to carry her backpack with her so Bear wouldn't come home, find it, and catch her,

Convincing Jenny to skip school had been more difficult than she thought. Every other period, her friend would come up to her with one whispered anxiety or another, wondering if it was the right choice and what would happen to them if they were caught. Mandy had stayed calm and confident the whole time. If she showed any kind of doubt, Jenny would've latched onto that and backed out for good.

Luckily for Mandy, the only thing Jenny loved more than school was learning about pirates. Twice as much if she could get hands-on experience. All Mandy had to do was bring up Blackbeard or ancient coins or mysterious shipwrecks, and the other girl's eyes would brighten and the plan would reignite.

She just hoped Jenny had stuck to her word and hid when the bus came to pick her up that morning.

As Mandy approached Jenny's house, she didn't see the other girl waiting for her. An empty car sat across the street. An older gentleman walked a pair of tiny dogs who yapped at her as she passed. Other than that, the street was empty. Her friend had abandoned her.

A bush rustled behind her, and Mandy jumped back a foot, planting her feet and raising her fists. When a little blonde head emerged from the leaves, she lowered her arms and crossed them over her chest. "Don't sneak up on me," Mandy chastised. "I could've hurt you."

"Sorry!" Jenny stumbled out of the bush, catching herself on Mandy and almost sending them both tumbling. "I wanted to be sure it was you before I came out."

Mandy peered into the bushes the girl had been hiding in. They looked pretty thick and leafy. "Can we stash our bags here?"

"I'm bringing mine." Jenny hoisted it higher up her back. "It has important stuff in it. Collection bags. Magnifying glass. Some books if we need to identify the coins."

Mandy groaned. The last thing she wanted to do was carry her backpack all the way to the beach, but if she lost her books, Bear would know they skipped. "Fine. Come on. Let's go."

It took Jenny almost an hour to lead Mandy to the spot where the most coins had been found. Mandy was just glad when they got there so she could drop her bag in the sand and stretch out her shoulders and legs. Despite all her training, they'd probably still be sore tomorrow. She had to make sure Bear didn't notice.

Jenny didn't look like she was in any pain, and her bag had to be twice as heavy as Mandy's.

As soon as they got to the spot, Jenny took out a couple bags, slipped one of the smaller books in her jeans pocket, and found a stick with a pronged end so she could move the sand around and look for treasure. All the while she kept up a steady stream of fun facts and interesting stories about pirates. Mandy tuned her out.

When Bear had told her they were moving to North Carolina, where he'd grown up, she thought they'd be inland. Maybe in the same house he'd lived in as a child. Bear didn't talk about his past a ton, and she'd never wanted to press him on it. Although, she was curious. More than curious. She wanted to know everything and anything about her dad. Sometimes it hurt her feelings that he didn't want to tell her, but sometimes she understood why it was easier to keep those memories locked away. That's what she did with her own childhood.

She'd been disappointed when she found out Hatteras was the destination, especially once she learned he didn't own the house he'd grown up in. Everything that Bear had ever touched was out of her reach. Part of her had hoped they'd get closer during their stay along the coast, but so far, that hadn't been true.

The opposite, actually. Bear never listened to her. He spent a lot of his time next door or with Rosie at the ice cream shop. And when he did pay attention to Mandy, it was usually to yell at her about something or other. She tried to be a good kid, really, but when you'd seen as much as she had, it was hard to sit still. Bear wanted her to be normal, but she knew she never would be.

She knew Bear loved her, and she understood what he'd sacrificed for her. He wanted them to have a normal life because he couldn't bring himself to lose someone else. Sasha was dead and never coming back. Jack Noble was gone, and while he was still among the living, there was a chance they'd never see him again. All they had now was each other. Mandy didn't want to lose that, but she couldn't just sit around and wait for Bear to tell her what to do next. She had to prove to him that she could handle herself.

"Hey," Mandy said, interrupting Jenny's latest tirade about maritime law. "Do you know anyone by the name Andrew Doyle?" Bear had only told her his name because he wanted her to look him up on Facebook. He didn't have a profile.

Jenny didn't seem bothered by the interruption, but she didn't look away from her work either. "No, I don't think so. Who's that? Someone famous?"

"No, someone who lives here. He's bald with a big chin."

"That's not really specific. My dad is bald with a big chin."

For a second, Mandy wondered if Andrew Doyle could've been Jenny's dad, but then she remembered she'd met Mr. Pickett and the two of them looked nothing alike. "I know. But that's what he looks like. Kind of scary."

"What about him?" Jenny asked, bending down to take a closer look at something and then tossing it away when she realized it was worthless.

"He keeps showing up. First at the ice cream parlor and then next door."

"At the Murrays'?"

"Yeah. Trying to figure out who he is. I don't think he'd a good guy."

Jenny looked up then. "There are lots of bad guys around here. More than people would think."

Mandy would've narrowed her eyes if they hadn't already been squinting at the sun. "What do you mean?"

Jenny shrugged and returned to her work. "I've heard my parents talking about how people don't really stay here anymore. *It's not like it used to be.*" Jenny did a perfect imitation of her mother. "I was always afraid we'd have to move, that someone would force us to sell our house like Tommy Gallagher's family had to sell theirs. My dad said that we live too far from the beach. No one would be interested in our house."

Mandy opened her mouth to ask Jenny what she thought her dad meant by that, but something else caught her eye. They had wandered far enough down the beach to get closer to the marshes. Jenny was convinced that because fewer people came down here, they had a higher chance of finding something valuable. Mandy wasn't so sure. The grasses were tall and there were scraggly trees everywhere. Each time Mandy took a step, she sank a little bit deeper in the sandy mud.

What had caught Mandy's attention was a bright flash of blue against the green and brown of the marsh. It was too high up to be the water reflecting back at her, but too far away for her to really see what it was.

Jenny caught her looking and turned around. "Do you see something?"

Mandy was already making her way toward the splash of color. Goosebumps trailed down her arms. She didn't really think they'd find any treasure today—she had just wanted to do anything other than be stuck in school.

It wasn't until Mandy hovered over the object that she realized what it was. Half-submerged in water and covered up by tufts of grass and broken branches, the bright blue paint had been covered with enough mud that it was hard to distinguish. Once the pair started brushing the debris clear, Mandy knew exactly what she was looking at.

"It's a boat," Jenny said, the wonder evident in her voice.

"No," Mandy replied. She couldn't hide her excitement either. "It's a submarine!"

11

BEAR HAD LEFT MANDY TO PUT HERSELF ON THE BUS THAT MORNING SO he had time to get over to Rosie's place before she headed out for work. She walked to work most days, rain or shine, unless there was a hurricane bearing down on them.

He had stopped over at the Murrays to check on Joseph too. The old man had a nasty bruise on his shoulder and hip, but Muriel—a nurse in a past life—was sure nothing was broken or fractured. Bear had wanted them to go to the hospital, but considering Joseph's pride, he didn't push.

It felt good to stretch his legs today. Yesterday's fight—or lack thereof—left him off-kilter. Doyle had been aiming to knock Bear down and out, and if he'd been anyone else, Bear would've eaten pavement worse than Joseph. He should've broken both Doyle's legs for even attempting to swing on him.

For the dozenth time since the incident, Bear wondered what was going on around the small town of Buxton. Between the family moving out of his old house in such a rush and the guy trying his damnedest to buy up the Murrays' place, someone was looking to get as much real estate around here as possible. Doyle had also seemed like an outlier until he showed up outside the Murrays'.

As hard as he pushed, Muriel and Joseph wouldn't tell Bear what was going on. Muriel had clammed up tight this morning when Bear tried to push, eyeing her husband like she was afraid of betraying him. Muriel never had a problem speaking her mind before, so Bear wondered what scared them so much that she'd keep her mouth shut now.

The air was cool this early in the morning, still warming up from the sun. Even in January, you could get away with a light jacket on most days. The breeze was chilly, but it kept Bear's senses sharp.

As he neared Rosemary's house, he saw her step outside and lock up. Whatever answers he didn't get from the Murrays, he was determined to get them from her. She knew more than she was letting on, and Bear had a feeling she'd be more willing to talk about it with him than his elderly neighbors were.

"Morning," Bear called out. He didn't want to spook her with Jed and Doyle lurking around every corner. "Mind if I walk you?"

Rosemary looked up, startled at first. When she saw it was Bear, a huge smile spread across her face. He swore it was brighter than the sun. Whatever happened between them and however they'd leave it behind—and they *would* leave it—he was glad to have known her, even for such a short amount of time.

"Hey, Bear. You're up early."

"This is nothing." He grinned. "Most days, I'm up before the sun. Old habit."

"From your military days?"

"Oh, yeah." Bear had told Rosemary shades of the truth. She didn't know the whole story, but she knew enough to understand what kind of person he was. "You want some company?"

Rosie nodded her head shyly. "I'd love it."

Bear fell into step beside her. "Have any trouble last night? Anyone come knocking?"

"No, nothing." Rosie tucked a strand of hair behind her ear. "Thank you again for everything. With the man at the shop. And with Jed."

"Speaking of," Bear began. He wasn't trying to be subtle here. "I ran into our friend from the shop again."

Rosie looked up at him and almost stumbled. "You did? Are you okay? Did he try anything?"

"He tried." Bear chuckled. "Wasn't too successful."

Rosie didn't look convinced. "What happened?"

"Heard some loud music outside my house and found him parked in front of the Murrays'. Joseph went outside to tell him to turn it down. Got a face full of concrete as a thanks."

"Oh my god! Is he okay?"

"Bruised up pretty bad, but Muriel said there are no fractures or anything worse. He was lucky, as far as I'm concerned."

"I should do something for them. Send you home with some ice cream one of these days. They don't come in as much as they used to, but I know Joseph used to love my salted caramel swirl."

"He'd have to be crazy not to."

"And you?" She looked him up and down, as if searching for injuries. "Are you okay?"

"He didn't get the chance to touch me," Bear assured her.

"Did you hurt him?" Her voice was quiet.

"Banged him up a little. Nothing major."

When she looked back at him, her eyes were hard. "Good."

"The name Andrew Doyle ring a bell?"

Rosie shook her head. "Is that him? The guy from the shop?"

"Yeah."

"They never tell us their names. They just come in and demand the money."

Bear didn't miss the way she said *us* and not *me*. He let the silence stretch between them for a moment. "This is starting to get out of control, Rosie."

Her eyes grew wide. Innocent. "What do you mean?"

"The Murrays getting harassed. You getting harassed. By the same guy, no less. Something's going on here, and I have a feeling you know more than you're letting on."

Rosie's voice was even, but she avoided eye contact. "I told you I have no idea who he is."

"But you know why he's there. The vandalism and all that." Bear let that sink in for a few seconds. "Has anyone ever tried to buy the shop from you?"

Rosie was quiet for so long, Bear was sure she wouldn't answer.

"Yes."

"When?"

"A few months ago."

"But you told them no." It wasn't a question.

"I wasn't going to give up everything I worked for. I put everything I had into building that shop." She sounded more than bitter. She was angry. "And they were lowballing me. By tens of thousands of dollars."

"And that's when the vandalism started?"

"Not right away. This guy, a real estate agent, kept coming around every couple of weeks. I kept telling him no. Then another man showed up. I thought he was just another customer at first. He came back a few times, always ordering ice cream and talking with me. He was nice."

"But?"

"He kept talking about how he'd always wanted to open up his own ice cream shop. I thought he was just someone who wanted to own their own business. I offered him tips. I thought we'd be friends. There's plenty of room for ice cream on the island. Plenty of customers. At least back then. But next he asked me how much I'd take for the shop. I told him it wasn't for sale. He got scary after that."

"Scary how?"

"All pretenses dropped. It was like his whole face morphed. He started threatening me with health code violations and other things that would drive away my customers. But I keep a clean shop. I wasn't afraid of that."

"What did he do when he realized he couldn't bully you into selling?"

"He left. A couple days later, the graffiti showed up. And not just on my building."

"All down the block," Bear supplied. They probably used the same tactic on all the businesses.

Rosie nodded. She blinked away the sun, and Bear wondered if she also blinked away tears. "That went on for a while. Then someone showed up to offer a deal. I'd keep my shop and they'd stop the vandalism. But it'd cost me."

"And you agreed." There was no accusation in Bear's voice. Just facts.

"I didn't really have a choice. I wasn't going to sell. I couldn't. But it was more expensive to keep fixing what they ruined than it was to just pay some guy every week to stop it from happening."

Bear didn't blame her. They'd backed her into a corner. Most people would've taken the money they'd offered, but Rosie loved making ice cream. She loved bringing people joy. And she also had nowhere else to go. Her entire life was on the island. She wouldn't leave without a fight.

"What's the name of the real estate agency that was harassing you?"

"I-I don't know."

Bear looked down at her. They were close to the shop now. He needed answers. "I need you to tell me the truth."

Rosie looked more hurt than angry, but she didn't deny it. "You shouldn't get involved, Bear."

"It's too late for that. Doyle knows who I am. It won't be long until his bosses know my name too."

"Which is why you should just drop it. There's no point in making it worse."

"It's going to get worse whether or not I'm involved. Some people are going to say no, like the Murrays, and the harassment will continue. And the more people who take the money, who pack up and leave, the more whoever is bankrolling this operation will feel entitled to the island. No matter which one plays out, both scenarios mean you'll be the last one standing. And that's not going to end well for you."

Another hard look passed through her eyes. "I can take care of myself. I'm not helpless."

"Never said you were." He saw the way she'd stood up to Jed and his friend. Rosie might not be the kind of girl to take a swing at someone, but she had her own kind of strength. She'd had every opportunity to leave her business behind, but she hadn't. That made her braver than a lot of other people who'd once called Hatteras home. "But it's good to have someone in your corner."

"I have people in my corner." Rosie put her hand on the doorknob to the shop but didn't twist it. "And we decided we weren't going to rock the boat. It's not worth it."

"And you agree with that?" Bear had seen the fire in her eyes when he'd told her he'd knocked Doyle on his ass. "You don't want to get to the bottom of this?"

Her eyes softened and turned sad. "I wish I could do something. But I'm not built for that." A little laugh escaped her mouth, and it was watery with emotion. "I just want to make ice cream."

Bear stepped closer. "Let me help you."

Her voice was quiet. "You're just one person."

"Sometimes that's all you need. Do you trust me?"

She looked up at him, and he could see her fighting with herself. She swallowed audibly and nodded her head. "Yes."

"Tell me the name of the real estate agency. I'm just going to ask some questions. Gather information. I want to know who we're up against. You don't have to do this on your own anymore."

Rosie smiled, but as much as she trusted him, Bear could tell she didn't believe he'd be able to change anything about her situation. "Rocky Pointe Realty."

A wave of relief passed through him. "Thank you."

She licked her lips, suddenly looking nervous. "Do you want to come over for dinner tonight? Maybe we can talk about what you found out?"

"Sure." Bear cleared his throat. "Yeah. That works for me."

Rosie pushed open the door and stepped inside. Right before she closed it behind her, she hesitated and turned to him. "Be careful, Bear."

Bear gave her his most confident smile. "Always am."

12

IT HADN'T TAKEN LONG FOR BEAR TO FIND ROCKY POINTE REALTY'S headquarters in Avon, north of Buxton. He never thought he'd say it, but thank God for Google. He was still slow—Mandy would've laughed at the way he pecked at each letter on the keyboard. He even found their website, proudly displaying each of their esteemed agents' photographs and bios.

He picked out the guy who'd shown up at the Murrays'.

Ethan Gray was a conventionally attractive man with thick brown hair and a bright smile. In fact, his teeth were so white, Bear was convinced they were fake. Or Ethan had paid a lot of money to make them look like that. His tanned face and sharp eyes made him look like the real estate agent who'd ensure you got the home of your dreams.

Bear had debated the best way to get this guy where he wanted him. If he gave Gray his information, he'd know he was the Murrays' next-door neighbor. There weren't any pictures of Bear on the internet, however, between Gray's own eyes and Doyle's description, they'd be able to put two and two together.

No, he needed the element of surprise on his side.

That's how Bear found himself driving north to Avon in the middle of the day. It only took half an hour, but the stretch along the beach made it feel longer. He'd grown up traveling these roads, but something instinctual about driving over the water made his knuckles turn a shade whiter on the steering wheel. His gut shouted at him to avoid going where predators lurked just under the surface.

Avon wasn't all that different from Buxton, though it was smaller. If nothing else, Avon boasted a larger grocery store, to which Bear had already traveled a dozen times to pick up dinner ingredients before Muriel had started feeding them.

He hadn't noticed the sign for Rocky Pointe Realty last time he was here. The headquarters was a small building. Unassuming. It looked like the rest of the local architecture, and despite the business's fancy website and host of elite agents, it didn't look like the agency was trying to rise above the rest of the community. In fact, when Bear walked to the front door, he saw a bulletin board boasting several events sponsored by Rocky Pointe.

Inside, a plump older woman with short gray hair and glasses straight out of the seventies sat at a desk blocking off the hallway lined with offices. She looked up with a hint of curiosity. Her accent indicated she had been born and raised in the Deep South. "Well, hello there, hon. What can I do for ya today?"

Bear plastered a smile on his face too. "Afternoon ma'am." He knew when to be tough and when to play the game. "I'm here to speak with Ethan Gray. Is he in?"

"'Fraid not." The woman frowned, as if delivering this news had ruined her entire day. "Can I leave him a message for you?"

"No, that won't be necessary. I'm an old friend. Just wanted to give him a little surprise."

"Oh, how nice!"

"You wouldn't be able to tell me where he is right now, would you? What house he's showing?"

This time, the woman wore a more uncertain frown. "I'm sorry, hon, but I'd get into a lot of trouble if I did that."

"Oh, I understand." Bear started moving before she even realized what he was doing. "I'm just going to pop into his office and leave him a message."

Whether she was shocked by Bear's boldness or unsure if she'd be able to stop him, the woman watched as Bear slipped behind her and stalked down the hallway until he spotted the plaque for Ethan Gray's office. He figured there was a fifty-fifty chance it was unlocked, and when it popped open under the gentle twist of the doorhandle, he found out luck was on his side.

"Sir!" The woman had gotten up from her desk, hand clutched to her chest in shock. "Sir, you can't be in there."

A head popped out of another office, but Bear slipped inside Ethan Gray's and shut the door behind him, then locked it. The secretary likely had a key, but he hoped having to unlock it would delay her long enough.

Gray's office matched his name—flat and boring. All the pictures on the wall looked like they belonged to a catalogue. Nothing had a personal touch, not even the frames on his desk. There were two large filing cabinets, probably locked. Bear didn't need to dig that far anyway.

A huge whiteboard nearly the entire length of the wall sat opposite Gray's desk. On it, the agent had written out the addresses of the houses he was showing and their market value, organized by date. Only one was listed for today.

Gotcha.

Just as the doorhandle started to jiggle, Bear crossed back over to the desk and ripped off a page from a yellow legal pad. Across it, he scribbled, *Murray,* and left it in the middle of the man's desk for him to find later.

Bear crossed the room and arrived at the door just as it opened. A young man was on the other side with the secretary hovering over his shoulder. The man looked up at Bear with a little fear in his eyes, but he managed to stammer out a few words. "Y-you shouldn't be in here when Mr. Gray is a-away from his office."

"Ethan and I go way back," Bear boomed, clapping the man on the shoulder and nearly buckling his legs. "We love playing little pranks on each other. He won't mind, trust me."

"I-I'm not sure—"

Bear slipped out of the room and down the hall with the other two on his heels. "Thanks for letting me drop my note off to him. Tell him to reach out when he's got some free time. He knows where I am."

And with that, Bear hustled from the building and back into his vehicle, pulling away from the curb and heading farther north. The address on the whiteboard wasn't far from the office. There was a good enough chance that the secretary had called him the second Bear left the building, and Bear didn't know the man well enough to anticipate how he'd react.

Turned out, Mr. Ethan Gray wasn't one to run and hide. As Bear pulled down the lengthy driveway of a three-story waterfront home, Gray welcomed him with a congenial wave. A couple in their fifties stood off to the side, both dressed in white with gold jewelry sparkling in the sun. Bear threw the truck into park and stepped into the fresh air.

"What a surprise," Gray said, sounding anything but. "I heard you might be on your way, but I told Belinda I wouldn't believe it 'til I saw for myself."

"Here I am." Bear spread his arms wide. He looked over Gray's shoulder and waved at the couple who had retreated into the shade along with presumably another realtor. "Hi there."

The woman waved back, but the men merely scowled in his direction.

"Mr. Logan, I have to admit this is not a good time for me."

"Oh, so you do know who I am."

Gray maintained his friendly exterior even as his body tensed. "Riley Logan. You live next to the Murrays. After our chance encounter the other day, I made it a point to look you up."

"Lucky me."

"Is there something I can help you with? As I said, this isn't a good—"

"As a matter of fact, yes." Bear kept his voice loud. He wanted Gray's clients to hear him. Even more so, he wanted the other real estate agent to witness their conversation. "I wanted to give you a chance to explain why you've been harassing my friends about selling their house. Don't you know that no means no?"

Gray's smile became tight as he called out to the others over his shoulder. "Please excuse me for a moment while I clear this up."

Bear allowed the other man to guide him by the elbow until they were just out of earshot. "Is there something you don't want your colleague to know?"

"I assure you, Brandon is more unscrupulous than I am." Gray dropped his fake smile. "I grew up in a household where we don't air out our laundry in front of complete strangers. Now." He looked Bear up and down. "Why are you here?"

"Leave the Murrays alone."

"You could've called me. Or simply left a note with my secretary."

"I wanted to make sure you got the message."

"Consider it received." Gray shook his head. "I've done nothing illegal or out of the ordinary. The Murrays have a beautiful home that would sell for more now than what they paid for it back in the sixties. It's in their best interest."

"It's in *your* best interest."

Gray shrugged. "I'm a salesman. It's my job."

"Is it your job to send thugs around to everyone who says no to you?"

"I have no idea what you're talking about."

"I met your friend. Andrew Doyle. Was it your idea to have him push around an old man?"

Gray didn't miss a beat. "I don't know anyone by that name. If something happened to Mr. Murray, I assure you I had nothing to do with it. I don't need to throw around my weight to close a sale." He raised a too-perfect eyebrow. "Can you say the same?"

"We all have our talents." Bear weighed his next options. He didn't want to mention Rosemary's name, but there was already a good chance this guy knew about her. "You deal in commercial real estate, too?"

"No. Residential only." There was still a light in his eyes, and Bear had a feeling this guy was smarter than he gave him credit for. "Does this have anything to do with the proprietor of a certain ice cream shop?"

"What do you know about that?" Bear asked.

"That maybe Rosemary isn't the person you think she is." He let that sink in for a moment before continuing. "Is that all, Mr. Logan? I have work to do."

Bear knew he'd get nothing more out of the man. He'd lost his element of surprise, and Gray was unflappable. Bear would have to find another tactic. Or another person to interrogate. He called out to the couple just a stone's throw away.

"You should buy it," he said, pointing to the house.

"Oh yeah?" The woman looked all too happy to have his attention. "Why's that?"

"I would never live in something as pretentious as this," Bear replied, "but it suits you well."

13

BEAR HAD COME HOME THAT AFTERNOON TO FIND MANDY ENGROSSED IN her homework. She claimed it was so she could go over to Jenny's house later that night, and Bear was inclined to believe her. Or maybe he was too distracted by his meeting with Ethan Gray to ask Mandy any penetrating questions. However, Jenny's parents had to make an unexpected trip to the mainland for some reason and wouldn't let Jenny have friends over. Mandy would be stuck at home. Bear had thought about dropping her off at the Murrays' while he had dinner with Rosie. Ultimately, he decided he didn't want to place anymore of a burden on them than necessary, what with Joseph still recovering.

That's how he ended up driving to Rosemary's with Mandy in the passenger seat. It was a short trip in the truck, and she found a way to complain the entire time.

"I don't understand why I can't stay home by myself."

"You know why." Bear fought to keep his tone even. He loved Mandy more than life itself, but that girl found a way to wind him up like no one else. Not even Jack Noble. "It's too dangerous right now. We're not taking any chances."

"I can handle myself."

"I know you can." She'd only said it a hundred times that evening. "I'm not risking it. End of discussion."

Mandy huffed and was silent for two blissful minutes. "I don't like this."

"I don't either," Bear said. He wasn't trying to be mean—he'd just been looking forward to spending some time with Rosie outside the ice cream parlor or a bar. And maybe figuring out what the hell Ethan Gray had meant by his line about not knowing who she really was. "But we can't always get what we want."

"Don't I know it."

Bear let the comment go as they pulled into Rosie's driveway and hopped out of his truck. The soft glow of the lights from within felt warm and welcoming—although Bear would've enjoyed it more if he couldn't hear Mandy grumbling under her breath right next to him.

Rosie answered the door almost immediately. Bear noticed that she'd changed out of her casual clothes from this morning and into a light green dress. The kind of thing she could run errands in, but more suited for a night out on the town. Bear suddenly felt underdressed in his t-shirt and jeans.

"Hey," he said, trying his damnedest not to follow every curve of that dress.

"Hi." Rosie's eyes landed on Mandy, and though her smile didn't falter, he caught the question on her face.

"Hope you don't mind I brought a plus-one." It was too late now if she did, anyway. "Her plans for the night fell through, and I didn't want to give Muriel one more person to look after."

Mandy didn't say anything, but he could hear her thoughts screaming, "I can handle myself!"

Rosie didn't bat an eye. She stepped to the side to let them in. "Not at all. I've got plenty of food." She looked down at Mandy. "How was school? Did you have a good day?"

Mandy could feel the way his gaze bored into the back of her head. Her answer was succinct but not unfriendly. "Pretty good. As good as school can get, anyway."

"I hear ya." An awkward beat passed while the three of them stood in the living room, wondering what to do next. Rosie took charge. "Mandy, would you help your dad carry everything out to the back porch? I've got a table set up there. I just need to, uh, grab something quick."

Bear watched her retreat to the back of the house before turning to the kitchen. Her home was small but comfortable for a single woman. The living room was big enough, covered in family photos and decorated with fluffy pillows and soft blankets. It was connected to a dining area, but Bear could see through the sliding glass doors to the patio where a table had been set with plates and wine glasses and a pair of flickering candles.

"Smells good at least," Mandy said.

Bear hummed in agreement, following his nose to the kitchen. Rosie had gone all out with roasted chicken, mashed potatoes, asparagus, and a couple bottles of red wine. It even looked like she had dessert on the counter under a piece of tinfoil.

"Come on." Bear picked up the roast chicken with two hands. "You grab the sides."

Mandy complied in silence, and they walked the food out back. With hot food and a nice glass of wine, he doubted they'd notice the slight chill in the air.

"You could've warned her, you know." Mandy sat down at the table and looked at the empty spot in front of her. Rosie had already set up plates and glasses for the two of them. "Way to make it weird."

Rosie chose that moment to step through the doors with one of the bottles of red wine. She was still wearing her green dress, now with a darker green cardigan over the top of it. Something told Bear that it wasn't just the chill in the air that had her rummaging through her closet.

"Oh, sorry, you need a plate, don't you?" Rosie set the wine bottle on the table and went back inside for Mandy's tableware. When she returned, she had a plate and a regular glass in her hand. "What would you like to drink? Water? Milk? I'm sorry, I don't really have other options."

"Wine?" Mandy reached for a stemless glass.

"Water is fine," Bear answered, giving Mandy a look.

"Water it is." Rosie came back with a pitcher and filled Mandy's glass to the top. "I think that's everything, yeah?"

Mandy cleared her throat quietly. "Could I have some silverware, please?"

"I'm so sorry! Yes, of course. Hang on." With a flushed face, Rosie stepped back inside and returned with utensils and extra napkins. "Anything else?"

Bear pulled out her chair. "I think that's all. Let's eat before it gets cold."

Rosie looked grateful as she slipped into her chair and started cutting up the chicken, plating everyone's food. She'd given Mandy an extra helping of mashed potatoes at her request, and Bear got a few extra slices of chicken. He poured them both wine and didn't miss the way she gulped down half her glass as soon as everyone had their plates in front of them.

Rosie opened her mouth at the same time Bear did.

"How was your—"

"Did you have a good—"

They laughed, and Mandy rolled her eyes at her mashed potatoes.

"Sorry," Rosie said. "What were you going to say?"

"Just wondering how your day was. Any customers?"

"One." She looked a little crestfallen. "They ordered vanilla. No toppings."

"Sounds like a lot of fun to be around."

"What about you? Did you, um, have a productive afternoon?"

Bear caught the way Mandy looked at him out of the corner of her eye. "Yeah, not bad. Not as productive as I wanted it to be."

"Sure. No problem." Another awkward pause. "What about you, Mandy? How was school?"

"You already asked me that," Mandy said.

"Right. I did," Rosie replied.

"Mandy," Bear warned.

"Well, she did."

Rosie placed a calming hand on Bear's arm. "It's fine. Sorry." She took a deep breath. "Have you come to like anything about Hatteras yet?"

"No." Mandy continued to pick at her mashed potatoes.

Rosie looked down at her plate for a beat. "Oh, that's too bad. I used to love walking along the beach to look for coins."

Mandy stiffened for a moment, then visibly forced herself to relax. "Bear won't let me go to the beach."

"By yourself."

"I'd go with Jenny."

"Without adult supervision."

"I'm fourteen, not eight."

"She's got a point," Rosie said. When Bear shot her a look, "I'm sure you broke the rules once or twice as a kid, didn't you?"

"I'd rather we not talk about that," Bear replied.

"I'd rather you did." Mandy set down her fork and leaned closer, placing her chin in her hands.

"This is really good, by the way." Bear held up a forkful of chicken. "What seasonings did you use?"

"Come on," Mandy groaned. "You never tell me anything."

"I tell you lots of things."

"Not what I want to hear."

"Secret family recipe," Rosie told Bear. Then she turned to Mandy. Bear knew she was happy to finally have something to talk about with Mandy. "I don't know about your dad, but when I was a kid—"

Whatever Rosie was going to say next was cut off by a deafening boom that shook the glasses on the table and sent all three of them diving to the ground.

14

REVERBERATION OF THE BOOM HUNG IN THE AIR.

Bear looked first to Mandy. Her eyes were wide. Hands shaking. Then he looked to Rosie. Her eyes were closed and both hands covered her mouth. Other than the shock to her system, she looked fine too.

Then Bear went through his own checklist, ticking off body parts one at a time. Head? Chest? Shoulders and legs? All fine. There was no broken glass and no screaming neighbors.

So what could it be?

Bear wracked his brain. When he landed on the answer, he couldn't help it. He started laughing. Loudly.

Mandy looked at him like he'd gone insane. Rosie peeked from behind her fingers like she was afraid she'd catch a glimpse of mangled body parts. Bear just kept laughing. Then he helped the girls to their feet. And laughed some more.

"What's so funny?" Mandy asked.

Bear sat back in his chair and started to cut off a new piece of chicken. "Sounded like a canon was heading right toward us, didn't it?"

"Yeah." Mandy sat down, too, but she didn't pick up her fork. "What was that?"

"They're called the Seneca Guns."

"A gun?" Mandy asked.

Bear shook his head. "Scientists aren't sure what they are. It's a natural phenomenon. Could be atmospheric. Could be related to earthquakes. Loud as shit, though."

"Yeah." Mandy laughed a little, but she still looked apprehensive. "Will there be more?"

"Not sure." Bear shoved a piece of chicken in his mouth. Strange as it was, the sudden burst of adrenaline had calmed him down. Taken some of the tension out of the air. "But probably not."

Rosie was still standing, looking out into her sunset-soaked backyard. "Are you sure?" She turned back to Bear. "Are you sure that's what it was?"

"Definitely wasn't an explosion." He heard plenty of them over the years. "Or a real gun." Those too. "Or a car backfiring. Only leaves one option, really."

"What if it wasn't?" Rosie asked. "What if it was something else?"

"Well, we're all okay, right? That's the most important part." Bear swallowed his chicken and put his knife and fork down. "You okay?"

"I-I just want to check the news." Rosie ran inside. "Just in case."

Bear and Mandy exchanged a look. Mandy's face clearly said, "What's with the nutcase?" Bear ignored it. He could still hear Ethan's voice ringing in his ears. He followed Rosemary inside, Mandy hot on his heels. They found her standing in the living room, one hand covering her mouth and the other flipping through channels on the remote.

"Rose?" Bear kept his voice quiet. Even. "Everything okay?"

"I just want to make sure."

They let her flip through channels for a solid five minutes before Bear walked over to her and gently took the remote from her hands. She backed up until her legs hit the couch, then she sank into the cushions. A tear dripped down her cheek.

"Will you grab her a glass of water?" Bear asked Mandy. It was a miracle Mandy didn't complain. She turned around and walked into the kitchen, opening cupboards until she found a cup. Ice clinked against glass a moment later. Then water poured in from a pitcher. A few seconds later, Mandy returned, handing it to Rosie.

"Thank you," Rosie said, avoiding eye contact.

"You okay?" Bear asked again.

Rosie took a sip before she answered. "Yeah. Sorry. Just got scared."

"What are you so shaken up about?"

Rosie's gaze flickered to Bear's face and away again. "I don't know. Just thought—" She cut off, took another sip of water, then cleared her throat. "It was so loud. Almost sounded like a bomb."

Maybe to the untrained ear, he thought, but he wasn't going to tell her that.

"Definitely Seneca Guns." Mandy held up her phone, showing Twitter. "Some people from school are talking about it. Even the local weather guy updated his status. Every time one goes off, it helps them get a little closer to figuring out what it might actually be. He sounds pretty excited."

Rosie made a non-committal noise and took another sip of water. Bear sat next to her Maybe the sound had triggered a memory from a past trauma. His body had wanted to have a similar reaction, until he'd realized the true source of the noise.

Bear's gaze slipped past Rosie and landed on a framed picture sitting on an end table. It was a group of three kids and their parents. Rosie's blonde hair and million-watt-smile were instantly recognizable. Another girl, a few inches taller, had darker hair and a more somber face. Then there was a young boy, older than both of them, with a goofy grin stretched across his face. He held up both hands in a peace sign, like he was incapable of posing without hamming it up.

The boy looked familiar. Once he recognized the kid, everything else fell into place. "Holy shit," he whispered.

Rosie's head snapped up. "What?"

"No, no. Sorry." He pointed to the picture. "You're Reed Callaway's little sister?"

Rosie picked up the picture and looked from the frame to Bear and back again. "How did you know Reed?"

"We used to hang out every summer. That kid was nuts." Bear turned to Mandy. "He used to jump off of anything and everything, like he was invincible. I think he was." He laughed. "Saw him hit the concrete more than once. Never broke anything. Always bounced right back up and kept going." Bear turned back to Rosie. "I remember you, too."

Rosie's eyes were wide, but not like they'd been before. "You do?"

"Quiet. Shy. We never hung out. You're, what, four or five years younger than him?" She nodded. "You'd always rather read a book than run around with us. You used to go by Mary back then."

"That's what my mom liked to call me." She scrunched up her face. "I never liked it."

"And your sister was Rhoda, right? She was only a year or two younger. She liked to hang out with us. Saw her deck a kid once. He cried all the way home to his mom. She got in so much trouble."

"I remember that." Rosie relaxed more now. "She was grounded for a week, but my dad was secretly proud of her. That kid wouldn't leave her alone. He had it coming." Her face scrunched up again. "Which one were you? I knew all his friends back then."

"Riley." He held out his hand, like they were meeting for the first time. "Riley Logan."

"Oh." She placed her hand in his, and they stared at each other for a few seconds. "Oh wow!"

"I filled out a bit since then."

Rosie took her hand back, but they kept staring at each other. "I guess so."

"How is Reed? What's he up to these days? I'd love to catch up. Does he still live here? I can't believe this never came up—"

"He's dead." Rosie looked back down at the picture of her brother. "Two years ago. He was murdered. We never found out who did it."

Bear swore under his breath. He heard Mandy gasp. "Rosie. I'm so sorry," He said.

Rosie set the picture back down on the table, adjusting it until it was perfectly in place. When she turned back to them, tears were streaming down her face. Bear opened his arms, and she leaned into him, shaking with sobs. He held her until she stopped crying. Even Mandy knew enough to let her get it all out.

15

MANDY WAS ACTUALLY EXCITED TO GO TO SCHOOL THE NEXT DAY. NOT because she was looking forward to *class*. Bear had told her over and over again how important school was and that you never knew what random piece of information could help you one day. But she couldn't bring herself to care.

Still, it was hard to hide her smile as she slid into her homeroom seat that morning. Jenny was already there, a conspiratorial look in her eyes. They had so much to talk about. The two of them shared a few classes throughout the day, mostly after lunch. And Mandy didn't want to wait.

"Did you hear it last night?" she asked.

"I think everyone heard it. It was hard not to. It was so—"

"—loud!" Mandy finished for her. Jenny nodded her head enthusiastically. "Scared the shit out of me."

Jenny clasped a hand over her mouth and looked around the room. She never swore, and she always looked so shocked when Mandy did. A light in the girl's eyes made it clear she'd secretly liked it. "It scared me, too. My dog went crazy!"

"Did you parents know what it was?"

Jenny bobbed her head up and down. "We've heard them before. But it still takes a few seconds for it to sink in. Our whole house shook!"

"I was over at Rosemary's with my dad." Mandy made a face. "Don't ask."

"I'm sorry you couldn't come over last night."

"That's okay. Is your grandma okay?"

Jenny nodded. "Yeah, she was fine. She keeps falling. I heard them talk about putting her in a home soon. Do you think they'll let her keep her cats?"

"I'm not sure." Mandy noticed the tears in Jenny's eyes. "But probably. I'm sure there are homes for the elderly that allow pets. Otherwise, where would the crazy cat ladies go?"

"My grandma is *almost* a crazy cat lady." Jenny said it so matter-of-factly that Mandy laughed. "Dad says one more cat, and they'll send her a certificate in the mail."

Mandy had to smother her laughter with a hand. A boy in the next row over looked at her, and she glared at him until he turned back around. "Rosemary totally freaked out," Mandy told Jenny. "She got really scared after she heard the boom. Like she thought something exploded."

"It was a pretty loud one," Jenny offered. "And it does kind of sound like an explosion."

Jenny liked Rosemary, but Mandy still wished her friend would be mad with her. There was just something about the woman that rubbed Mandy the wrong way. She was too nice. And in her experience, nice people were always trying to get something from her. She just hoped Bear was being cautious. "I guess."

After a minute of silence, Jenny changed topics. "Did your dad find out we skipped school?"

"No." Mandy's eyes went wide. "I was so scared. But he was too distracted." Mandy lowered her voice. "He's up to something, but I don't know what. Or where he went yesterday while we were" —she lowered her voice even more— "you know where."

"I can't stop thinking about it." Jenny was almost hysterical with glee. She had never broken a rule in her life, and the adrenaline was getting to her. "Should we go back?"

"Definitely." Mandy stayed calm. Tried to look older and wiser, even though Jenny's birthday was before hers. She had more experience with this sort of thing. "We should go back at night and have a sleepover in it."

Jenny sobered. "I don't know if that's a good idea. It can get really dark out there sometimes."

"It's supposed to be a full moon tonight." Mandy had been thinking of this plan for hours, and she knew Jenny would be afraid of the dark. "We'd have plenty of light to see by."

"Do you think that's safe?"

There was an element of danger, but Mandy wasn't about to tell Jenny that. "It's not like we're going to try to drive the submarine or whatever it is out to sea."

They had opened the hatch and looked inside. There was some water in the bottom, but there were two perfectly good beds. For some reason the mattresses were missing, but that didn't matter. Jenny had sleeping bags they could use instead. "I just want to pretend we're anywhere but here."

"It's not so bad here," Jenny said.

Mandy shrugged. "I guess." She looked out the corner of her eye at her friend, not even trying to hide the wicked smile on her face. "We can pretend to be real pirates."

That caught Jenny's attention. "What do you think it was used for?"

"I don't know. Maybe spy stuff." Neither one of them had wanted to go inside yesterday when they found it, for fear of being caught, but when Mandy had stuck her head inside, it had looked empty. "Or maybe even modern-day pirates."

"It's definitely possible."

"Definitely possible," Mandy repeated. She had her friend hooked. Now she just had to reel her in. "Think of it as research. We can live like pirates for a night. You bring the sleeping bags. I'll bring the snacks."

"Pirate snacks?"

"Um. What did pirates eat back then?"

"Biscuits. And jerky. And probably beans."

"My dad has some jerky! And we have rolls. Do those count?"

"Close enough." Jenny thought for a moment. "I'm pretty sure my mom has a couple cans of beans in the cupboard."

"We'll have to eat them cold," Mandy said. "We probably shouldn't start a fire."

"What if we get cold?"

"I'll bring some blankets too." It was harder for Mandy to keep her voice down. "This is going to be so much fun."

Jenny looked worried. "We're going to get caught."

"Ask your parents if you can sleep over at my house tonight. It's Friday, and you don't have to do anything tomorrow, right?" Jenny shook her head. "And I'll ask my dad if I can go over to your house. He'll probably let me since I couldn't come over last night. We'll meet at the end of your street and go straight to the beach."

"And we can set an alarm on our phones so we wake up early—"

"—in time to get back so no one knows we're missing. It's perfect." Mandy was grinning like a wild woman. "It's gonna work."

Jenny opened her mouth to respond, but Mandy never found out what she was going to say. Another boom rocked the little town of Buxton. This one didn't shake the windows, and it sounded farther away. There was no mistaking that Mandy had heard it. All the kids sat up straighter.

"More Seneca Guns?" someone asked.

While most of the class discussed it amongst themselves, Mandy turned to the windows. Her gut was telling her something was wrong. All the lights in the classroom flickered and went out.

That's when the screaming started.

16

BEAR KNEW THE SECOND HE HEARD THE BOOM.

That was a real explosion.

He'd been sitting at home, contemplating whether he should pay Ethan Gray another visit, when the sound jolted him from his chair. His body recognized it before his brain did. Unlike last night when the adrenaline kicked in and cleared his head, this time it muddled his responses. He stood stock still for thirty seconds, waiting for another one.

Silence.

Bear took the stairs two at a time and sprinted to his bedroom at the end of the hall. He wrenched open the closet door and pulled out the lockbox on the top shelf. Punched in the code. Pulled out his gun. The weight calmed him. Only one thought filled his brain.

Mandy.

That was enough to drive him from his room, back down the stairs, and out into the chilly morning air. It was another clear day, but there were clouds on the horizon. There was no one on the street.

Joseph must've seen Bear on the sidewalk. He poked his head out the front door. "That was real."

"I know." Bear waved him back inside. "Lock up. I'm going to get Mandy."

Joseph didn't argue. He slipped back inside, and Bear got into his truck, taking another thirty seconds to regulate his heartbeat. He could feel his palms sweating, his mind running away with impossible scenarios. *Terrorist attack*, his brain whispered. He shook it loose as another thought occurred to him. *They've found you.*

Bear didn't know who *they* were, but he'd survived this long by assuming someone was always out to get him.

Except it wasn't just his life on the line now. It was Mandy's too.

Bear threw the truck into drive and pulled away from the curb, overcorrecting one way and then the other. So much for regulating his heartbeat. He slowed down and focused every cell in his body on getting to the school. It wasn't far from the house, but he wanted his truck in case they needed to get away quickly. North Carolina Highway 12 was a straight shot out of there.

Bear pulled out his cell and called Mandy. It rang five times before going to voicemail. He swore. Then he hung up and called the school. It was busy. He hung up and tried again. Same result. He tossed the phone into the passenger seat and swore again.

Bear only noticed the dark traffic light a few feet from the stop line on the road in front of it. He slammed on his brakes, nearly colliding with a small Toyota that beeped angrily at him. He threw a hand up in apology, then checked both ways before continuing straight through.

Whatever happened, it had cut the power off to the island.

Bear squeezed his hands against the steering wheel. His chest tightened. He'd come to Hatteras to escape, and now it felt like a trap. A single island amongst a whole ocean.

He punched the steering wheel but slowed enough to make it through the next intersection without almost hitting anyone. More people gathered in the street now. More cars, too.

He wondered what Mandy was thinking. Did she think it was the Seneca Guns? Did the other kids know better? What about the teachers? Would they tell the students what was going on, or would they play it off to keep them from panicking? Mandy was too smart not to figure it out. She'd realize something else was going on.

Mandy was a strong girl. Tough. Smart. She wouldn't panic. He had drilled scenarios like this into her mind over and over. *Don't be a hero. If you can help someone else, do it. But not at the risk of your own life. Let the adults do their jobs. Let them protect you. But don't let your guard down.*

Not that Bear trusted anyone else to protect his daughter. That list was short. It started and ended with Jack Noble. These days, even that was a last resort.

Bear pressed his foot down on the gas, urging his truck to go just a little bit faster. He didn't bother with his turn signal as he whipped around a corner and slammed on his brakes. There was a line of cars in front of him. And they were at a complete standstill.

Bear swore again, then checked his mirrors. First the rearview, then the driver's and the passenger's sides. Another car pulled up behind him, beeping its horn. Bear threw his hands up. What did they expect him to do?

Bear waited until the line inched forward enough for him to pull off to the side and get out. It wasn't a good parking job, but it'd have to do. He was only a few blocks away from the ice cream store. He'd be faster on foot at this point. Maybe he could borrow Rosie's car. It was smaller. He might be able to get through traffic faster. Part of him knew it wouldn't help, that he just had to be patient, and the other part felt like he was in a warzone. He'd do anything to get to his daughter.

Rosie was standing outside her shop when he arrived. She spotted him first and ran up to him, stopping short of throwing her arms around him when she spotted the look on his face. "Are you okay?"

"Mandy." He had to force her name out between breaths. "I have to get to the school."

A man standing a few feet away turned to him. "The school? Did something happen at the school?"

"My daughter. I have to get to her."

"It's okay." Rosie placed a hand on his arm. "It wasn't the school."

Bear shrugged her off. "I have to get to Mandy. Where's your car?"

"At home. I walked."

Bear cursed. Of course she did. She always walked. He'd have to go back for his truck. He turned to leave, but she caught his arm.

"Hey, what's going on? Talk to me."

Bear was panicking. He couldn't let Mandy see him this way. That was the only thought that kept him rooted to the spot. He closed his eyes. Took a couple deep breaths. Looked down at Rosie. "Sorry. I just— I need to get to Mandy. I need to make sure she's okay."

Someone gasped from behind him. "Oh my God! Look."

Bear turned to the woman, then followed the trajectory of her pointed finger. North. Toward Avon. Away from the school. Black clouds in the sky, the wind carrying them higher.

Still, the tightness in his chest eased a little. He still wanted to make sure Mandy was okay.

He turned to Rosie. "I have to go."

She nodded her head and let him slip back to his truck. He rejoined the faster-moving traffic. Nothing felt like slow motion anymore. And fewer than ten minutes later, he was in the school parking lot.

Bear ran to the front doors and yanked on the handle. Locked. He pressed his face to the glass and cupped his hands around his eyes. Almost jumped back when he saw another face staring back at him. The security guard was shaking his head.

"I'm here for my daughter," he yelled through the glass. "Mandy Logan. Let me see her."

The man shook his head again. Bear growled. He was sure it was something about protocol and locking the school down and not letting anyone in or out for the safety of the kids, but his lungs squeezed tighter, and the panic made him throw all logic out the window. He banged a fist on the door in frustration. Some kids were still in the hallway behind the security guard. A few turned in his direction.

Then one broke free from the crowd and sprinted to the door. Before the guard could stop her, Mandy pushed it open and leaped into Bear's arms. He could've cried with relief. He squeezed her tight, feeling the air whoosh out from her mouth and a quiet giggle tickle his ear.

"Bear, you're crushing me."

"Sorry." He set her down, then looked her over. "You okay?"

"Yes. Are you?"

He nodded. "Scared the shit out of me."

"What was that?" she asked. "It sounded different."

"Explosion. From Avon, I think. Not sure what's happening."

Mandy lowered her voice so the security guard couldn't hear her. "Is it—"

"I don't think so, but we can't be too careful." He stood and looked the other man in the face. "I'm taking my daughter home. If you need me to sign something, I suggest you find the paperwork. Now."

17

BEAR HAD DOZENS OF QUESTIONS FLOATING AROUND HIS HEAD, BUT THE top two were 'what happened and why?' He could answer at least one with a short drive north, but he wasn't about to drag Mandy any closer to the site of the explosion.

The school had let him sign her out, and soon more parents showed up to take their kids home. Even if they'd stayed in school, there wasn't much they could do without power. Plus, no one would be able to concentrate with all the excitement. They didn't know what was going on, but rumors were flying faster than ever.

"I'll stay at the Murrays," Mandy offered.

Bear shot her a look. They were on their way back from the school now. "Why?"

"Because it makes the most sense." Mandy shrugged. "I know you want to check it out, and there's no way you're going to let me go with you, is there?"

"Not a chance."

"Exactly. You're not going to let me stay home alone either, are you?"

"Not if I can help it."

"I'll help Mrs. Murray cook dinner, and maybe after I can go to Jenny's for the night? Then you won't have to worry about me."

"Have you suddenly matured, or are you up to something?"

Mandy placed a hand on her chest and scoffed in mock offense. Then her face sobered. "I want to know what's going on too. You have to tell me if you figure it out. That's the deal."

"We'll see," he said, but she had a point. Having her stay with the Murrays was the best course of action. "But you call me if anything happens. Especially if anyone shows up to harass them again. Call. Do not engage."

"Sir, yes, sir." She even saluted.

Bear laughed, and some of the discomfort in his stomach unknotted itself. When he arrived back home, he checked in with the Murrays, who were more than happy to have Mandy around. Muriel had already pulled out some candles and board games, and Bear had seen Mandy's eyes light up at Monopoly. They'd be entertained for a few hours, minimum.

And just like that, he was heading north to Avon. Most people were off the streets now, back home with their families.

He'd only been traveling on Highway 12 for a few minutes before he came across a road closure. A few cars had parked along the side of the road, and he pulled off behind them. He was just south of Kite Point now, and it didn't take a genius to figure out someone had used the narrow strip of land to their advantage.

Walking the shoulder the rest of the way, Bear encountered a group of onlookers pressed against a barricade the police had erected. Still, from a couple hundred yards away, and with the acrid smoke hanging in the air, Bear knew what he was looking at.

Ahead of him, someone had taken a small boat from the Pamlico Sound and either driven it or pulled it up into the middle of the highway and detonated it with enough explosives that it had flooded the road and cut them off from Avon and the mainland.

And it wasn't just the highway. The power and telephone lines had been damaged too. They were dead in the water.

Bear inched closer, not wanting to bring any attention to himself, but letting curiosity get the better of him. The boat had been completely destroyed, but there were some pieces scattered across the undamaged highway that might allow police to identify who it once belonged to. Unless, that is, the bomber had been smart enough to cover their tracks.

From where he stood, he couldn't tell what kind of explosive it had been. No dead bodies lay around—either whole or in pieces. Chances were high that it had been remotely detonated. Not as hard as you might think, but still more than what was in the average person's skillset.

Someone had purposefully blown out this strip of the road—chosen because of its narrowness—to isolate them. But why? Bear was sure it wasn't because of him and Mandy, as much as his paranoia wanted him to think otherwise. Regardless, this was a warning. A big one.

Bear looked over at a man next to him, neck craning to get a better look. He held a pen and pad of paper in his hands. A reporter. "You know what happened? Have they said anything?" Bear asked.

The man shook his head, not taking his eyes off the damage in front of them. "No one was hurt. At least as far as they can tell." He looked down at his paper, where Bear saw scribbles that might've been words. "Lots of C-4 packed in there. Did a lot of damage. Gonna take some time to repair the road."

"Power too, probably."

The man nodded. "We're in for an interesting couple of days."

Bear didn't like the sound of that. "They have any suspects?"

The man finally looked up at Bear. "Don't think they'd tell us that if they did."

"True, but you must have thoughts."

The reporter turned back to the site. "Lots of strange things going on around the island this year. Most of the news is usually about tourists getting lost or petty theft, that sort of thing."

"What kind of strange things?"

Bear saw the man stiffen a little. "Not sure. Probably nothing. My mind likes to connect dots that aren't always there." He looked at his watch. "I should get back and write this up."

Bear let the reporter go, even though he wanted nothing more than to push for answers. He probably wrote for the *Island Free Press*. Bear would be able to find him again if he needed to.

Until then, he had a few more hours to kill. He'd stick around here to see if anything else turned up, and then he had one more stop to make. Ethan Gray might've been trying to sow seeds of doubt in his brain, but given Rosie's reaction to the Seneca Guns, something told Bear she knew a hell of a lot more than she was letting on.

18

BEAR TURNED UP ON ROSIE'S DOORSTEP WITHOUT A PLAN OR AN IDEA OF what he wanted to say to her. She answered almost immediately when he knocked.

"Bear." She sounded surprised. And a little nervous. "Everything okay? How's Mandy?"

"Mandy's fine." He was glad for the question. It gave him something else to focus on for a few seconds. "School let me sign her out. She's home with the Murrays."

"Good. And you?"

"Me?"

She shuffled from foot to foot. "How are you?"

He decided to bite the bullet. "Can I come in?"

She hesitated for a few seconds, then stepped to the side. "Okay."

Bear walked in and made a beeline for her couch. He sat down, looking around as if trying to spot something out of place. Something that would tell him he was on the right track. Everything was as tidy as usual. Even the picture of Reed was still in the same spot he'd found it last time. A laugh bubbled up at the improbability of their connection, but he pushed it down. Bear didn't want to upset her again. He just wanted some answers.

"Can I get you something to drink?" Rosie asked. It was just a formality. "Water? Coke?"

"I'm good." He really wanted a beer. "Thanks, though."

"You're kind of freaking me out." She let out a nervous laugh, then stood in front of him. "What's going on? Is something wrong?"

"I visited the site of the explosion. Just got back."

Rosie blanched. "What? Why?"

Bear shrugged. "Wanted to know what was going on."

She seemed to accept that answer. "What was it?"

"Somebody detonated a boat full of explosives on the highway. Cut us off from Avon."

Rosie closed her eyes and rubbed a hand over her forehead. "Why would someone do that?"

"You tell me."

She opened her eyes. "What? Why would I know?"

Bear studied her for a moment. She was wearing another dress. Light and flowy. Made her look even more delicate. Like a light breeze could sweep her away at any second. The denim jacket looked warm, and not like something you'd wear around the house. It took a Bear a few more seconds to realize she might've been on her way out.

"Going somewhere?" he asked.

Rosie looked at him pointedly, like she knew what he was up to but would indulge him for a few more minutes. Maybe. "Meeting a friend." She waited to see if he had another question. "Why would I know why someone would blow up the highway?"

"The other night. The Seneca Guns. You were scared."

"It was loud," she said. "I don't like loud noises."

"Your first thought was to check the news. To see if something had happened."

"That's a very normal response, Bear." She was starting to get angry now. Little splotches of red crept up her neck. "It sounded like a canon. You said so yourself."

"You've lived here your entire life. That's not the first time you heard them." He didn't wait for her to answer. He already knew. "Yet your first thought was an explosion went off. Like you'd been waiting for it to happen."

"What exactly are you accusing me of?" Rosie folded her arms across her chest. "I was at the ice cream shop when it went off. You saw me."

"Doesn't mean you don't know something." He leveled her with a look. "Who set off the bomb, Rose?"

Several emotions flickered across Rose's face. Anger. Fear. Maybe even something like hope. When she spoke again, her voice was quiet. Tiny. "I don't know."

"Rose—"

"I really don't know, Bear. That's the truth."

"But you have an idea, don't you?"

"I—"

There was a knock at the door. Rather than looking surprised, Rosie looked defeated. When she crossed the room, Bear stayed put. A few seconds later, Rosie returned with a man. He was tall with broad shoulders and a tanned face. And he looked vaguely familiar.

"Zeke, this is Bear." Rosie gestured between them. "Bear, Zeke."

Zeke looked at Rosie, as though he wasn't expecting them to have a third wheel. Out of politeness, he held out his hand. "Hey, man."

As soon as Bear heard his voice, he knew why he looked so familiar. "Hey." He shook the man's hand. "We've met. You were helping someone move out of their house."

"The Sampson's, yeah." Recognition lit up his eyes. "You used to live there, right? You had your kid with you."

"Mandy, yeah."

The air was heavy with an awkward beat of silence before Zeke broke it. "I feel like I'm interrupting something."

"You aren't," Rosie said.

At the same time Bear admitted. "A little bit yeah."

Rosie shot him a look. "Bear was just leaving."

"I was?"

Zeke looked uncomfortable. "Look, I don't want to cause trouble—"

Rosie laid a hand on Bear's arm—a warning—but she spoke to Zeke.

"You're not. Bear and I can finish our conversation later." Rosie turned to him. "Tomorrow morning? You can walk me to work again."

Bear dug his heels in. He wasn't sure if it was his urgent need for answers, or the fact that he was afraid Rosie would keep finding ways to avoid him. Not that she had anywhere to go with the highway shut down. "I'd rather talk about this now."

Zeke looked at his watch. "If we don't leave soon, we're going to be late."

"Off to catch a movie?" Bear asked. He regretted the quip as soon as it left his mouth. He wasn't a jealous person, not usually, but emotions had been high over the last twenty-four hours. He couldn't stop what came out next. "Power's still out, so can't be that."

"It's not like that," Rosie said quietly.

Zeke held up his hand. There was a gold band on his ring finger. "Married, man. It's just a town meeting."

"Oh, so I can attend, then." Maybe he'd get some answers that way.

"It's kind of invite-only."

Bear looked between Zeke and Rose. Whatever was going on here, both of them knew something. Before he could press further, Bear's phone went off. He wanted to ignore it, to keep pressing for answers, but if it was Mandy—if it was an emergency—he'd never forgive himself.

Turned out, it was Mandy. There was no emergency. Just a quick text message.

Can I go over to Jenny's? Pleeeeeease??

Before Bear could answer, Jenny's mom was calling him. He picked up on the second ring. "Mrs. Pickett. How're you doing?"

"You know, hanging in there." She was a quiet, intelligent woman. Bear had only met her once, but she seemed like a good person. Both of Jenny's parents did. The girl had drawn better lots than Mandy, that was for sure. "You heard about the road?"

"Yeah." Bear wanted to ask her questions, too, but he was aware of both Rosie and Zeke's stares. "You good with the girls spending the night?"

"Fine with me, if it's fine with you."

"Sounds good. I'll see you in the morning, then." Bear hung up and texted Mandy.

You can go. But be careful.

Thank you!!!

You need a ride?

Mrs. Murray said she'd take me! Thank you!!

Bear sighed and shoved his phone back in his pocket, then stood from the couch and looked down at Rose. "Tomorrow morning. Answers."

"I promise." Rosie looked like she meant it, but she also looked like she just wanted him out of her hair. "I'll tell you what I can."

Zeke looked like he wanted to say something but thought better of it. Bear took that as his cue that he'd get no more out of either of them tonight. Without saying goodbye, he left.

If there was ever a time for a drink, this was it.

19

BEAR WALKED INTO TEACH'S TAVERN WITH A CHIP ON HIS SHOULDER AND a point to prove, which was good news for the bartender and bad news for the crowd. It was packed tonight, probably because the bar was the only place on the island with a backup generator. What else was there to do when the power was out?

He found a spot at the end of the bar where he could watch the townsfolk laugh and shout and whisper about what had happened. The island rarely saw this much action, and none at all during the winter months. They'd make the mainland papers for sure. Maybe even the national news. Some lived for the drama, and others just wanted it to all blow over.

But Bear caught snippets of information. Whether or not they were true, he had no idea.

"I heard it was a terrorist attack."

"Then why didn't they kill anyone?"

"I heard it was a disgruntled electrical worker."

"Did you ask your cousin where he was this afternoon? Ha ha ha."

"Heard it was the *Citizen's Brigade* firing a warning shot."

"Shut your mouth about shit you don't know about."

That caught Bear's attention. It was the first piece of information that had sounded like it could've been real. He didn't know what the Citizen's Brigade was, but that second voice clearly hadn't wanted his friends to talk about it. And what was better?

That second voice had belonged to none other than Rosie's ex—and Bear's new best friend—Jed.

Bear was four beers deep now. On a good day, that would've been light work. Today had not been a good day. The alcohol, high emotions from the bomb, and confronting Rosie had made Bear reckless. He ordered another round and swaggered over to where Jed and three of his friends were huddled in a booth.

"Fellas." Bear tipped an imaginary hat at them. "How's it going?"

All four of them looked up at him. One wore an actual cowboy hat. It was Roy, Jed's friend from the other night. He spoke first. "Piss off, man."

"Jed, come on, tell them I'm cool."

"You heard the man," Jed said. "Piss off."

"You're not still mad about the other night, are you?" Bear feigned his regret. "I'd really like to be friends."

"Fuck you."

"Ouch." Bear took another swig. "Fine, okay, I have to earn it. That's fair. Good old fashioned bar brawl?"

Roy shook his head, but his buddy in the red flannel spoke. "You don't want to do that, man."

"I think I do." Bear dropped his act. Stared Jed straight in the eyes. "Here's the deal. You tell me what this is about the Citizen's Brigade, and I'll walk out of here. Or I can beat the shit out of you, and you tell me anyway."

"It's made up, dude," Red Flannel said. "Just a joke about some resistance group on the island. They're not real."

"I kind of think they are." Bear didn't look away from Jed. "What do you say? We got a deal?"

Jed leaned forward. "Piss. Off."

"Too bad. I think we could've been friends." Bear dug his phone out of his pocket and held it up so they couldn't see the screen. "Sorry, gotta take this. It's Rosie."

Then he walked out of the bar.

It was a cheap shot, but that was the glory of a sucker punch. It caught the enemy unawares. And it had the added benefit of actually working.

Less than thirty seconds later, Bear found himself out back, surrounded by Jed, Roy, Red Flannel, and the other guy he decided to call Lazy Eye. For obvious reasons. The other three hung back while Jed stepped up to Bear, no fear in his eyes.

"Stay away from Rosie."

"She can make her own decisions."

"You don't know what you're getting into here, man," Jed hissed. "I'm trying to do you a favor."

Bear didn't care. He just wanted to blow off some steam. "Tell me about the Citizen's Brigade."

"It's not your concern."

"I'm making it my concern. Did they blow up the highway? Does Rosemary have something to do with it?"

Jed must've learned from Bear's tactics because instead of answering, he threw a right hook that connected squarely with Bear's cheekbone and sent him stumbling until he hit the building's wall. It took him a second to clear his head and spit out a wad of blood where he'd bitten the inside of his cheek. But the shot had sobered him.

Game on.

Bear pushed off from the siding and pretended to stumble, opening himself up for a shot he knew Jed would take. Tightening his stomach muscles, Bear let the man connect with his gut while bringing his right knee up and pushing the other man's head down until the two connected. He heard a satisfying crunch right before Jed howled in pain and sagged to the ground.

No rest for the wicked.

Roy and Red Flannel both came at him while Lazy Eye checked on Jed. Now that Bear had a closer look, he could see the resemblance between his two opponents. Definitely brothers. Maybe even fraternal twins. He noticed the identical shape of their noses before he threw a jab that almost broke Roy's.

With a growl, Red Flannel launched himself forward, wrapping his arms around Bear's waist in an attempt to throw him off balance. It didn't work. Bear picked up the other man with a roar of anger and threw him to the ground. Just in time for Roy to recover and throw a right hook and a left jab. Bear dodged one and caught the full brunt of the other, but it didn't set him off balance. He was in his element now.

With Jed getting to his feet, Bear knew he'd have to thin the herd to gain the upper hand. When Roy came in with another jab, Bear grabbed his wrist and twisted until the man yelled, then brought his arm up behind his back until the shrieking got louder. As Roy continued to thrash, Bear drove him headfirst into the side of the building, where he crumpled to the ground like a rag doll.

As Bear predicted, Red Flannel wasn't about to let that slide. He got to his feet and attempted to put a boot through Bear's chest. A quick step to the side and a well-placed kick to the knee insured that the man was down for the count.

The sound of a blade snapping open had Bear whirling around in time to see Lazy Eye slash at him. The tip of the knife caught Bear across the forearm, and he hissed in pain. It was enough to open up his skin, but not enough to do major damage.

As Lazy Eye brought his arm back for round two, Bear stepped close and pulled his knee up into the other man's groin. When Lazy Eye doubled over, Bear took the time to bend his hand back until the blade dropped to the ground. Then he kicked it far enough away so no one could grab it.

Lazy Eye looked up just in time to see Bear bring his elbow down against his temple. Then it was lights out.

That left Jed, his nose spewing like a faucet. The man spit out a wad of blood before walking up to Bear.

"What the hell is your problem, man?"

"Wish I knew." Bear was still riding high on the adrenaline of the fight, but his senses were starting to come back to him. Along with his conscience. "You gonna tell me what I want to know? Or you gonna get three more of your friends to jump me."

"You started this, man. Not me."

"You started it when you didn't take no for an answer."

"I'm just looking out for Rosie." Jed spit another wad of blood to the ground. "She doesn't have the best taste in men."

"Clearly."

Jed charged forward with his finger extended like a knife. When Bear stepped into his path, the man backed up and took a moment to compose himself before saying, "She likes to give people the benefit of the doubt. Even when it hurts her in the end. I'm not gonna apologize for thinking you wanted something out of her like the others."

"And you don't want anything from her?"

Jed held up his hands in surrender. "Can't help but dream. I don't always say the right things, and yeah, I miss her. I'm never gonna not love that woman. It makes me stupid. And angry. I never hurt her." He rushed on, and Bear felt awkward, like Jed was carving himself open in front of him. "Would never do that. But yeah, I get jealous. It's just my nature. Try to leave her alone like she wants, but I still worry about her."

"You're talking about the guys harassing her."

Jed shook his head. "Told her to pack up and leave. It'd be safer, but she refused. Loves that goddamned ice cream parlor too much. She'd do anything to keep it safe."

Bear raised an eyebrow. "Anything?"

"Not like that. She wouldn't."

Bear was inclined to agree, but something still wasn't right. "What's the Citizen's Brigade?"

"A stupid made-up name for a group of people who don't know when to leave well enough alone."

"You know more than that."

"So what if I do?"

"I think Rose is mixed up in something she's gonna regret. I'm not here to cause trouble. I care about her too."

"That's what they all say."

Bear shook his head. "I'm not looking to buy. I just want to keep my kid safe. Can't do that with roads exploding and my neighbors getting bullied out of their house. And yeah, Rosie paying thugs to keep her property safe. I don't want to stir up the mud here, man, but you gotta give me something. Things are just getting worse."

Jed sat with that for a full minute before he said anything. "They meet every Friday night, back of the deli. You can only get in with a password at the door. Only people who've been vetted get the password."

"You know it?"

"Had my privileges revoked." He swept his arms out to the side. "Talk to Rosie if you want to get in."

Bear thought about pressing for more information but decided he'd done enough damage for tonight. It all came back to Rosie, anyway. She was the one with answers. And now that he knew where they were meeting, he'd be able to do a little reconnaissance to get a leg up the next time they talked.

"Thanks, man. Appreciate it." As Bear walked away from Jed and the three men groaning on the ground, he hooked a thumb over his shoulder, back toward the bar. "Tell them next round's on me."

20

MANDY'S BODY BUZZED WITH ENERGY FROM THE TOP OF HER HEAD TO THE tip of her toes. On one hand, she was terrified at being caught, but on the other—the bigger hand—was alive with excitement. No wonder Bear was always sneaking off to places. This was *fun*.

Jenny had tried to pull out of the plan several times, but Mandy would redirect her attention back to some fun fact about pirates or some benefit of going on a midnight adventure. It wasn't always easy, but in the end, Jenny wanted to do this as much as Mandy did. And it was high time that girl lived a little.

The simplest part of the plan had also been the trickiest. She'd texted Bear—not trusting her voice to give away the lie—to ask if she could go over to Jenny's. Then, Jenny asked her mom if she could go over to Mandy's. It was classic for a reason, though a little touch and go when Jenny had said her mom *called* Bear. But they must not have talked long because a few seconds later, Bear had given her the green light.

Mandy had showed the Murrays Bear's initial text message. They let her walk out the door without any further questions, and before she knew it, she was meeting Jenny at their usual spot. From there, it was a hike back to where they had originally found the submersible. This time it took a little longer as they were laden down with the proper supplies.

Jenny was a few feet ahead, leading the way with some crazy inner compass that Mandy didn't possess. The other girl remembered exactly where they had found the submersible, even though they'd covered it up with even more vegetation to hide it from prying eyes. She said it was easy because it was just below Bald Point, but Mandy wouldn't know where that was if someone had a gun to her head.

"Hey, slow down." Mandy tried not to show she was out of breath. "Where's the fire?"

"Don't want to be seen," Jenny panted. "One good thing about the road being closed, I guess."

Mandy looked ahead to where the explosion had taken place farther up Highway 12. The smoke had mostly dissipated, but darkness enveloped the area, and she could see flashing blue and red lights from this distance.

"How much longer?" Mandy asked. She wanted to get out of sight too. She knew Bear had visited the explosion earlier, but he'd moved on. She'd be in serious trouble if he caught her on his way home.

"Just ahead."

Mandy had borrowed a pair of rainboots from Jenny, and she was glad to have them. They'd taken a slightly different route through the marshy area along the beach, trying to stay out of sight.

As soon as they came upon the submersible, Mandy forgot her wet feet, her sore back, and her tired limbs.

The little sub was right where they had left it, under the cover of copious vegetation and just downhill from the road so they'd be hard to spot. Even though the thing had been painted blue, it was muddy enough that it blended right into the background.

The girls dumped their bags in the driest spot they could find and checked the sub over from tip to tail. It didn't look too damaged, but they could only see the top two thirds of it.

Mandy was brave enough to scuttle up the side of the sub and twist the handle on the top, opening the hatch and leaning back in case anything jumped out. She waited for a count of ten before sticking her head inside to make sure it contained nothing alive.

"Well?" Jenny asked from the ground.

Mandy leaned back and scrunched up her face. "Empty. But it smells."

Jenny retrieved a bottle of Febreze from her bag and tossed it up to Mandy. "Use this."

Mandy looked from the bottle to Jenny. "Seriously?"

Jenny shrugged. "Figured it might've been here for a while. Could be moldy." Jenny brushed something off her sweatshirt. "Besides, if we get into something gross, I'd rather come home smelling like that so our parents don't suspect anything."

Mandy grinned. "You're a genius." She spritzed the inside of the container a dozen times, then waited another minute and did it again. "I think we're good."

Jenny climbed up the side of the sub, and Mandy helped her reach the top since she was a little bit shorter. When the other girl was in place, Mandy dropped down, wincing as her feet made contact with the metal floor and the sound reverberated around her. Nothing moved in response, but she didn't let her guard down.

"There's a car coming," Jenny hissed. "I'm not sure if they can see me."

"Jump." Mandy turned back to the opening. "I'll catch you."

Jenny didn't hesitate. She slipped inside and let Mandy stabilize her before the pair of them grinned at each other. "We did it."

"We did." Mandy looked around the little room. There were two empty cots with no mattresses, plus an empty bucket that had something dark stuck to the bottom that she figured was probably the source of the smell. A little opening led deeper into the boat. "What is this thing?"

Jenny looked at the navigational equipment near the hatch. "This is all in Spanish."

"Can you read it?" When Jenny shook her head, Mandy headed toward the back. "I'm gonna see what else is in here."

"Wait for me." Jenny scrambled to catch up, her feet slipping a little on the wet floor.

Mandy caught her just in time. "Do you think this sunk and washed up to shore?"

"Probably not." Jenny looked around the empty cargo area at the back of the ship. "They don't usually wash up this far onto shore. Not without a big storm."

"So maybe someone drove it up here?"

"Maybe."

Mandy thought that was pretty cool. But she was still disappointed there wasn't really anything to look at in the back of the boat. "You really think this could've been used for spy stuff?"

"Definitely." Jenny grinned. "Maybe modern-day pirates!"

A light splashing sound drew their attention back to the hatch. It had started raining. "Let's grab our packs. I'll bet we can translate those signs by the wheel."

Jenny's eyes lit up like Mandy knew they would, and the two scrambled out into the light rain, grabbed their stuff, and climbed back inside. Jenny had the wherewithal to make Mandy stay outside to test whether they could open the hatch from inside, and when it worked, they started setting up their stuff.

They'd each get their own bed with a sleeping bag and thin blanket to cushion against the metal springs. It wasn't comfortable, but it'd be enough to sleep a few hours before they headed back home. Mandy had brought a few games, and Jenny had brought some books, but they only had the light of their flashlights to see by.

Still, this was what Mandy had hoped for when she'd convinced Jenny to do this with her. They spent an hour or so translating Spanish into English, but when they didn't uncover anything too interesting, they spent the rest of the time telling scary stories. Mandy had never had a sleepover before, and there probably wouldn't be another one that could top this one.

When they set their alarms to go off prior to sunrise, Mandy didn't think she'd be able to sleep with all the adrenaline running through her veins. Jenny was already snoring lightly across the room from her, and it wasn't long before Mandy felt her eyes drift closed, too.

Despite the stiff bed, she was happy and content with their adventure.

At least until she awoke to the boat rocking and cold water splashing onto her face. Jenny screamed for her to wake up. Mandy fumbled with her phone until the flashlight turned on, then she squinted against the harsh light. Jenny already had her phone out, with the flashlight turned on, but it still took a few minutes for Mandy to comprehend what she was seeing.

Water. Lots of it. Enough that it was at least a foot deep.

And that rocking motion. What did that mean? She was almost afraid to find out.

Almost.

Jenny was crying now, but Mandy remembered how Bear would center himself before he had to do something big, like rescue a friend or fight an enemy. She took three deep breaths, then jumped down into the water, not thinking about how wet and cold it was.

She scrambled up the ladder and turned the wheel on the ceiling to open the hatch. When she popped her head out into the freezing cold air, rain whipped her face until it was numb. She wished she had stayed in bed.

Because she couldn't see the road.

Or land.

Or even the marsh.

Everywhere she looked, they were surrounded by water.

21

BEAR PARKED THE TRUCK A BLOCK AWAY AND ACROSS FROM THE DELI. RAIN poured onto his windshield, but he was still close enough to see anyone coming or going. He was certain Rosie was inside with Zeke and at least half a dozen others. The parking lot was full despite the sign on the front door reading *Closed*.

A dark neon sign adorned the small building's front, advertising fresh bread. Bear had eaten at the place a few times. The spicy Italian sub was out of this world, mostly in part to that bread. The owner was a guy named Sal. Nice dude, but Bear was starting to rethink some of his opinions.

Had they really detonated the road as a warning? The purpose of the explosion was to knock out power, but who had that benefited most? And who had it hurt?

Bear was itching to get inside that building. There was no way he'd be able to without getting caught. He thought about walking right up to the door, knocking on it, and spouting off some bullshit password like *Pizza* or *Calzone*. Maybe *Cannoli*. If Rosie saw him on the other side of the door, would she vouch for him? Would they let him into their secret club?

He debated the pros and cons of breaking up their meeting when his phone buzzed. Jenny's mother again. He almost didn't answer. Then again, maybe it was a sign from the universe. *Stay in your truck*, it said. *Don't stick your nose where it doesn't belong.*

The call almost went to voicemail before Bear finally picked it up. "Hello?"

"Thank God." She leaned away from the receiver. "Charles, he answered."

"Marissa?" Bear didn't like her tone of voice. "What's wrong?"

"I-I realized Jenny forgot to take her pills tonight. I called her to let her know I was going to run them over to your house. But she didn't answer."

"My house?" Bear asked.

"I decided I'd just pop over for a second, drop them off, and be gone. I didn't want to embarrass her or anything." The woman was hysterical now. "But it's not good for her to skip dosages."

Bear was still trying to wrap his head around the situation. "You went to my house?"

"Yes. But no one was home."

"Mandy told me they were spending the night at your house."

There was a sharp intake of breath from the other side of the phone. "Jenny said she was spending the night over there."

Bear cursed loud enough that Marissa couldn't have possibly missed what he said. He hit the steering wheel with the palm of his hand, then closed his eyes and took three deep breaths. Where could Mandy have gone? What the hell could she have gotten herself into?

Then another thought occurred to him.

Did someone take them? The girls had obviously played their parents, but why hadn't Jenny answered her phone? Could it have been Doyle, still pissed about Bear beating the shit out of him? Or Jed? Maybe the deli meeting had been a ruse to get Bear off his back long enough to take matters into his own hands. Then there was Ethan Gray. Physical intimidation might not be his usual M.O., but Bear couldn't trust anyone.

Marissa was shouting into the phone now. "Bear? Are you still there?"

"I'm here. I'm here." He took another deep breath. "You have any idea where they could've gone?"

"No, I—"

A double beep sounded in his ear, and Bear pulled the phone from his face. "Hang on," he said to Marissa, trying to reach her through her hysteria. "Mandy's calling me. Stay on the line." He didn't wait for an answer. Relief and anger flooded through him. "I'm going to ground you until you're twenty. Where are you?"

"Not now," Mandy snapped. Wind howled in the phone. "I don't know where I am." A sob escaped. Her voice was quieter now. "Bear, I'm scared."

"Take a deep breath." He waited for her to follow his instructions. "Tell me what you see."

"Nothing." She gulped down air. Steadied herself. "Water. I just see water."

What the hell? "You're on a boat?"

"Kind of. It's a submarine."

Bear's heart skipped a beat. "Did you say a submarine?"

"We found it in the marsh. By the side of the road near Great Island." Another sob escaped. "Bear, I'm so sorry."

"Don't worry about that now." Right now, he just wanted to get his daughter home safe and sound. "Are you in the Sound?" This time his heart stopped altogether. "Or are you in the ocean?"

"The Sound, I think. But we can't see any land."

"Jenny's with you? Are you hurt?"

"No, we're fine." The wind whipped against the speaker. "Just wet and cold."

"You can't see any land at all?" Bear tried to keep his hopes up, but they could be anywhere. "Any points of reference?"

Mandy was silent for a few seconds, and Bear pictured her taking her time to look around her, trying to spot something—anything—that would help. "I-I don't see anything. It's raining too hard and the waves are too high." There was a sharp intake of air. "Bear, find my phone."

"What are you talking about? You're on your phone."

Mandy growled in his ear. "No! Find My Phone. It's an app. It'll help you locate me." She paused. "My battery is almost dead. I can't stay on the line."

"Find My Phone. Right." He remembered that now. Mandy had protested when they first turned it on to connect their phones, saying it was a breach of privacy "This is what you're going to do. Are you listening?"

Bear could hear the concentration in her voice. "Yes."

"We're going to get off the phone, and you're going to preserve your battery. Anything you can do to make sure it lasts as long as possible. Do you understand?" He waited for confirmation before he continued. "I'm going to track you. Tell Jenny her parents are coming too. We'll be there soon. No matter what happens, you keep yourselves safe, you got it? Just hang on. We're coming."

"I love you, Bear."

"I love you too." Bear waited until Mandy hung up. When her line went dead, the call reconnected to the Picketts. Bear could hear them yelling and crying in the background. "They're both okay," Bear said. Their hysterics shut off. "They're on some sort of boat or sub in the water. Mandy thinks they're in the sound. Do you have a boat?"

"Yes." It was Mr. Pickett. "Down by the docks."

"Meet me there in ten minutes. I'm going to track Mandy's phone. We'll find them."

Mr. Pickett didn't acknowledge Bear's demand before he hung up. Bear trusted they wouldn't leave without him, though. They had to work together to get their daughters back.

All hesitation about disrupting the deli meeting went out the window as Bear kicked open his truck door and ran across the street in the rain. It was cold, and Bear could only imagine it was even chillier on the water. If Mandy and Jenny were soaked to the bone, it wouldn't be long before their bodies went to extreme measures to keep them alive.

With that on his mind, Bear rounded the back of the building and banged on the door. He wasn't trying to be subtle. When the murmured voices cut off, he knew they'd heard him loud and clear. But no one came to the door.

He banged again. "Rose," he shouted. "Rose, open up." Seconds ticked by. Too long. Too slow. "Rose, it's Mandy. She's in trouble. I need your—"

The door whipped open. Rosie stood there, confusion and panic warring on her face. "What's wrong?"

"Mandy and Jenny." Bear fought to keep his voice steady. "They got swept out to sea."

"*What?*" Rosie looked beyond him to the rain falling in sheets from the sky. "Where?"

"Not sure." Bear stepped inside, forcing Rosie to take a step back. It was warm in here. He was aware of his clothes dripping rainwater all over the floor while the group stared up at him. Bear recognized Zeke but couldn't name anyone else. He'd seen most of them around town. "I need you to help me find her phone so I can track it."

Rosie took his phone from his outstretched hand, her fingers flying over the screen. Within seconds, she pulled a map up. Sure enough, there was a little blue dot—Mandy's position in the middle of the Sound. She wasn't too far from shore, but in this weather, there was no way she could know that.

Bear looked up at Rosie. Whatever was going on between them—and whatever had been happening in this room minutes ago—it didn't matter. He was grateful. "Thank you. I'll let you know when—"

"No." Rosie grabbed her coat off the back of the chair and slung it on. She charged past him. "I'm going with you."

Bear knew there'd be no point in arguing, even if he wanted to.

22

MANDY HAD NO DOUBT THAT BEAR WOULD COME TO RESCUE THEM JUST IN the nick of time, but it was still hard to remain calm. Between the rain and the waves and Jenny's sobs, Mandy could hardly hear her thoughts. She felt the panic coursing through her body like she'd touched a live wire.

After she hung up with Bear, she lowered herself back into the boat, where she found Jenny huddled on her bed, clutching her backpack to her chest, and rocking back and forth. Even in that short amount of time, the water level had risen another six inches or so. It was just lapping at Jenny's feet now.

"Bear's coming for us." Mandy forced her voice to stay even. If she'd been alone, she might've started to cry. But Jenny was counting on her. Besides, this was all Mandy's fault. She had to assume responsibility. She had to make sure they stayed alive long enough to be rescued. "We're going to be okay."

Jenny just kept sobbing.

Mandy splashed across the room and grabbed the bucket floating in the corner. She held it out to Jenny. "We need to stay above water as much as possible." The boat rocked and almost sent Mandy tumbling back into bed. "I need you to scoop up water and hand it to me so I can toss it out."

Jenny looked between Mandy and the bucket. "That's not going to work for long."

"We don't need it to." She kept her voice gentle. "Just long enough for Bear to find us."

"How's he going to do that?" Jenny stood and took the bucket. She left her backpack on the bed, where it was already getting wet.

"He's tracking my phone." Mandy made a show of putting her phone in her pocket. "I put it on low battery mode. It should last long enough for him to get here. Your parents have a boat, right?"

"Yeah."

"They'll probably use that to come get us. It's going to be okay."

Jenny closed her eyes like she was in pain. "We're going to be in so much trouble."

"I know, but we'll deal with that later."

The fact was, Mandy didn't want to think about it. Bear was going to kill her. He'd ground her for the rest of her life. He'd never let her leave the house again. She'd have to pee with the door open, so he knew she wasn't trying to escape.

As the boat rocked from side to side one more time—knocking them both off their feet this time—Mandy wasn't sure she cared. She promised God or whoever was listening that if Bear found them in time, she'd try her hardest to stay out of trouble from here on out.

Jenny helped Mandy to her feet, then scooped up a big bucket of water. Mandy climbed the ladder until her head and shoulders stuck out of the opening. Then she grabbed the handle on the bucket and tossed the water overboard. There was nothing left to do but drop the pail back down to Jenny and repeat the process until someone came to get them.

Mandy wasn't sure how much time had passed since she'd last talked to Bear. Ten minutes? Twenty? The storm seemed to get worse. The sky was an angry gray. Lightning flashed in the distance. She didn't want to think about what would happen if it struck the sub. And the rain was so cold. She could no longer feel her fingers, and her clothes were so wet that if she stepped onto a scale, she'd probably weigh twice as much as normal.

They kept bailing water out of the sub one bucket at a time. Mandy tried to use her body to shield the opening, thinking she could stop at least some of the rainwater from coming in. It hardly made a difference, but it made her feel better.

Mandy attempted to get her bearings again. But the rain was so heavy that she could hardly see ten feet in front of her. Bear could be out there right now, merely a couple dozen feet away, and she'd have no idea. It gave her a glimmer of hope for a split second. Then she realized that he might have the same problem—he could be a few feet away and pass her by without ever knowing it.

"My arms are getting tired," Jenny said, holding up a full bucket once more.

It could've been the tenth or the millionth one, Mandy wasn't sure. She looked down to give Jenny some encouragement, but she shouldn't have taken her eyes off the water. There had been a few waves that knocked them around, spraying Mandy with saltwater and adding to the water level in the boat, but she'd kept a vice-like grip on the hatch opening and so far, she hadn't had trouble hanging on.

This wave was different. She felt its presence and had enough time to look up at the towering wall of water before it crashed down on them. Mandy never had a chance. She lost her grip on the hatch, and her feet slipped from the ladder. She fell and landed right on top of Jenny. Mandy got an elbow in the gut, and she was afraid she might've broken her friend's legs. But the real problem was that now Mandy didn't know which way was up. They were both underwater, turned this way and that by the rocking of the ship.

For a moment there, they were nothing but flailing limbs and racing hearts.

Then they broke through the surface, first Mandy, and then Jenny. Gasping breaths followed by shouts of fear. Mandy swore. Jenny cried. The saltwater stung their eyes, but they managed to find their way over to the ladder, clinging on for dear life.

"Are you okay?" Mandy shouted. The storm outside sounded so much louder now.

"I-I don't know."

"Anything broken?" Mandy did a mental survey of her own body. She'd probably have a bruise on her stomach, but otherwise she felt fine. "Anything bleeding?"

"I don't think so." Jenny squinted up at the hatch, the rain pelting her face. "It's getting worse."

Mandy looked around their little makeshift room. Both of their backpacks were underwater now, along with the waterlogged sleeping bags. The pail was empty enough to float, but it was just out of reach. Not that it mattered. There was at least three or four feet of water inside the boat now. Every time another wave crashed on top of them, it got worse. It was only a matter of time now.

Jenny looked back at Mandy. Her eyes were wild with fear. "What do we do now?"

"We need our backpacks." Mandy had brought some things with her that she couldn't lose. "I'll get them. You climb the ladder. Hold on tight, okay? Don't go outside yet."

Jenny nodded and started her ascent. Mandy waited until her friend was secure before she dove under the water, sweeping her hands out in front of her until they brushed one of the backpacks. She surfaced, saw it was Jenny's, and handed it up to her. Then she dove again. Another minute passed, but her hand locked on one of the straps. Jenny's had been heavier, but even her own bag felt like it weighed fifty pounds as she tried to pull herself up the ladder. Her limbs were so tired.

Another wave crashed down on them, and Jenny's foot slipped and landed on Mandy's fingers. She cried out, but only succeeded in swallowing more water. At least neither one of them had lost their grip.

"Are you sure this is a good idea?" Jenny yelled over the water. "It's safer inside."

"We need to be able to flag Bear down," Mandy said. She pulled herself up next to Jenny. With their backpacks on, the space was tight, but they were secure. "It's worth it to make sure he doesn't miss us."

"What about your phone?" Jenny asked. She wiped water from her face. Not that it made a difference. "It got wet."

Mandy groaned and pulled her phone out from her pocket. She tried turning it on, and the screen lit up. Thank God new phones were water resistant. Still, between that and her dwindling battery, it wouldn't be long before it was nothing more than a paperweight.

"How long do you think—"

Jenny never got to finish her question. Another wave reared up like a monster and crashed down on top of them. It bashed the two girls together and against the opening of the hatch. Mandy knew she'd have bruises along her ribs now. But that wasn't the worst part.

When the water finally receded and they could breathe again, Mandy realized her phone was no longer in her hands. She whipped her head around, looking left and right and everywhere she could, but the ocean had stolen her device.

Every second that ticked by meant they were being pulled farther away from the beacon Bear would be tracking.

They were officially lost at sea.

23

BEAR WAS SOAKED TO THE BONE. THEY ALL WERE BEFORE THEY HAD gotten into Gordon's thirteen-foot Boston Whaler. The storm made it difficult to see a dozen feet in front of them. Jenny's father was adept at driving his boat, but even he couldn't dodge every wave that reared its ugly head.

The two men were at the front of the boat. Bear held his phone so the other man could see, and they did their best to drive straight toward the dot on the map. Neither bothered speaking.

Meanwhile, Marissa and Rosie sat in the back of the boat, arms hooked to hold each other in place. Both clung to the boat for dear life, but Bear could see Marissa's wild eyes searching the water.

The fierce look of determination on Rosie's face never wavered. Bear was grateful for her help with the phone. He would've figured it out eventually, albeit slower. It was better that she was here. One more person to be on the lookout for Mandy.

Once again, Bear wondered what was going on with Rosie. They hadn't talked about the meeting, but Bear would have to tell her how he knew where she was. Whatever Rosie was mixed up in, it had something to do with both the explosion and the real estate agency's penchant for throwing its weight around. Now he just had to figure out how Doyle fit into all this, and what he could do to protect Mandy and the Murrays. And Rosie, if she let him.

Another wave crashed over the front of the boat, hitting Bear square in the face. He braced for impact, but his hand slipped from the back of the chair. He went down to one knee, pain shooting up his leg. Gordon's hand shot out and grabbed a handful of Bear's jacket, dragging him back to his feet.

Bear nodded his appreciation. He planted his feet better and wiped off the surface of his phone, holding it out in front of them.

They were close.

Bear figured they were coming up on Mandy's location within the next minute. He dug back into his memory to see if she'd shared anything important about the boat. She'd called it a submarine, but she clearly wasn't underwater. It would be bobbing on the surface as long as it hadn't gone under.

His heart jumped to his throat, then fell down to the pit of his stomach. If the boat went under, Mandy would be free-floating in the water. She was a good swimmer, but he didn't know about Jenny. Then again, the best swimmers got pummeled by the waves and dragged along by the current.

Gordon shouted something and Bear turned back in his direction, shaking his head. He couldn't hear him. Gordon pointed at the phone, and Bear looked down. They were on top of the blue dot.

So, where were the girls?

Bear handed the man his phone and leaned over the side of the boat, trying to peer through the rain to see if he could spot a flash of something—anything—that indicated Mandy was close by. He didn't see her.

Panic ensued. Maybe the GPS was off enough that the location wasn't accurate. Or she might've dropped her phone. Or she'd been pulled under the waves.

Bear was about the launch himself off the ship and look for her in the water when he heard something in the distance. Had that been a shout? A scream? Between the wind and the water and the motor, maybe his mind was just playing tricks on him.

"Cut the engine," Bear roared. Gordon shook his head, so Bear made his way back over to him and shouted in his ear. "Thought I heard something. Cut the engine."

The man did as he was told. The two women in the back of the boat stood up, bracing themselves again wild tossing, looping their arms around the metal framework for the boat's canopy, doing anything they could to stay on their feet.

The wind still whipped against Bear's face, and he thought he heard something again. A noise that didn't quite fit with the rest of the landscape. Totally out of place.

Then another sound came from his right. Bear looked over. Rosie was pointing in the distance, angled about thirty degrees away from where they were heading. Bear following her outstretched arm. A flash of blue in the water. Then a splash of purple. The color of Mandy's winter jacket.

The boat's engine roared back to life. Gordon turned slowly so he didn't risk hitting a wave wrong and flipping them over. It was taking too long for Bear. The girls could be swept further out. Swept under. His body filled with adrenaline. He whipped off his jacket and his sneakers. They'd just weigh him down.

The group arrived to where they'd seen the flash of blue. Just under the surface, sinking ever deeper, was a small submersible. Not exactly cutting-edge technology. By the way it was sinking, Bear figured it had a leak. A big one.

What about the flash of purple? Bear looked farther out. Just before his visibility cut off, he saw it again. Two heads bobbing in the water. One struggling harder to stay above the surface. And they were drifting farther out.

Bear turned and locked eyes with Gordon. The man nodded his head. He'd watch Bear. He'd follow him. He'd make sure the boat was ready. It was all the go-ahead Bear needed. He dove into the water without wasting another second.

The rain had been cold, but the ocean water was even colder. It was a shock to his system, and if Bear hadn't already been prepared for it, he might've lost his concentration. He was so close now. The girls were within reach.

Bear stayed under as long as he could, heading in the direction he'd last seen Mandy's jacket. As soon as he hit the surface, he'd be buffeted by the waves. They might even turn him around. He had to use his current momentum to keep his trajectory. If he messed up now, all three of them might be lost.

He had to come up for air. He swam toward the surface and gasped, trying to minimize the amount of seawater he swallowed. He looked around him but didn't see Mandy's jacket anymore. The current pulled him. The waves threatened to push him back under.

He heard shouting and turned. Rosie and Marissa were pointing off to his right. He turned and looked. Mandy was closer now, using her remaining strength to keep Jenny's head above water. Jenny was swimming as hard as she could toward Bear. He put all his remaining strength into cutting through the water. He had to trust the others to keep their eyes open.

Bear got to Jenny first, and she threw her arms around his neck. She was so light that it hardly made a difference. In those few seconds, Mandy slipped farther away, the waves pushing her down and making her disappear for a few seconds at a time. She always came back up sputtering.

Only when Bear got closer did he realized she still had her backpack on. That's what was pulling her down. Why hadn't she tossed it? She tried to protest when he slipped the straps from her shoulder, but Bear was stronger. He let it sink to the bottom of the Sound as he pulled his daughter close to him and wrapped her arms around his neck, above Jenny's.

He turned around to see the boat. Gordon cut the engine and threw a line out to Bear. He caught it and started to reel in. Rosie lowered the stairs at the back of the boat, then hauled Mandy and then Jenny up. She went back for Bear. He collapsed on the floor next to Mandy, who crawled over to him and laid her head on his chest. He was exhausted and grateful and so relieved that tears slipped from his eyes, mingling with the water still streaming down his face.

They still had to make it back to shore, but the hard part was over.

Mandy and Jenny were safe.

24

WHEN THEY MADE IT BACK TO SHORE, THE TWO GROUPS SEPARATED without so much as a word of goodbye. Bear caught Mandy staring after Jenny as she was hauled away by her parents, but the other girl was too busy being smothered to notice. He loaded his daughter into the back seat and cranked the heat as high as it would go.

They made it home in record time and went off to strip out of their wet clothes. There wasn't much for Rosie to wear, but they found one of Mandy's oversized band shirts and a pair of leggings that were far too short.

Mandy had climbed into a sweatshirt and a pair of sweats, wrapped a robe around her body and curled up under a blanket in the armchair. Her hair was still wet, so she was shivering, but the teeth chattering was at a minimum now.

Bear grabbed another blanket from the closet and tossed it to Rosie, who looked at him gratefully. Then they sat on the couch opposite Mandy, silent. Bear wasn't sure what he was feeling. Relief outweighed his anger. He knew more of that would come later when the adrenaline wore off and he had a chance to really think about how close it had come to disaster. Not just for Mandy, but Jenny, too.

If something had happened to either of them, Bear wouldn't have been able to live with himself.

Mandy's sobs broke through Bear's dark thoughts. She was staring straight at him, tears running down her face, trying to pull air into her lungs. He could see her eyes going glassy, like she wasn't fully present. The panic attack was taking her to a place Bear had never wanted her to go.

He slipped from the couch and knelt in front of her, unburying her hands so he could hold them. They were still ice cold. He rubbed them between his and told her it was going to be okay, to focus on her breath, to let him keep her safe.

"I-I'm so sorry." She hiccupped, a sure sign that the panic attack was passing. "I didn't mean for that to happen. I was so stupid."

"Hey, hey." Bear pressed his forehead to hers, chuckling when she hiccupped and they banged heads. "There's a difference between being stupid and doing a stupid thing."

More tears fell down her cheeks. "I did a stupid thing."

"You did, but we all have. I sure as hell have." Bear couldn't even begin to list the amount of shit he'd gotten into at her age and all the years since. "It's going to be okay. You're safe now. Jenny's safe now."

Mandy closed her eyes. "Jenny."

Rosie spoke up from the couch. "I'll check in with her parents. Make sure she's okay."

Bear was grateful for the space. He waited until Rosie walked into the kitchen, and then he waited for Mandy to look at him. "Tell me what happened. Get it off your chest. You'll feel better."

"A couple days ago, Jenny and I skipped school." She couldn't meet his eyes. "We walked along the beach, then into the marsh. We wanted to look for coins. Jenny's obsessed with pirates."

Bear remembered Mandy being excited about all the fun stuff Jenny was teaching her that they weren't learning in school. He also remembered letting it go in one ear and out the other. If he'd paid more attention, would she have felt the need to act out like this?

"But we found that sub. I thought it would be cool to spend the night in it, out by the water. Have a real sleepover."

"Sleepovers don't usually take place in submersibles." Bear said.

Mandy blew out a breath of air—the closest she could come to a laugh in her current exhausted state. "I know. I just wanted an adventure. This place has been so boring." She looked at Bear now, dead in the eyes. "I know that's not an excuse."

Bear leaned forward and kissed her forehead. "What happened next?"

"We got into the boat. It was pretty cool. There were beds in there but without the mattresses. Jenny had sleeping bags. We explored for a while. Everything was in Spanish. What was that thing, Bear?"

"Not sure." But he had a couple ideas. "I'd need to know what else you saw in there."

"It was pretty empty. But I have pictures."

"Your phone is at the bottom of the Sound, honey."

Mandy's eyes drooped, then opened again. "They're in the Cloud."

"Okay." He wasn't sure what that meant, but he wasn't going to worry about it now. "What next?"

"We went to bed for the night. Set our alarms for early so we could make it back without being caught."

"But then the storm started," Bear pushed. He wanted to get this out of her while it was still fresh. "You never checked the weather?"

Mandy shook her head. "It was stupid. I can't believe I forgot. I was just so excited. I woke up, and there was water inside the boat. And we were rocking back and forth. I was so scared, Bear. There was a bucket. We tried to get the water out, but it was coming in so fast. And the waves were getting bigger. We had to give up and just hope you found us in time."

"And I did." Bear made her look at him. "You did a good job keeping yourself safe. And you kept Jenny alive too."

"I'm in big trouble, aren't I?"

"Oh yeah." Bear wouldn't to sugarcoat it. "But we'll talk about it in the morning, okay?"

"Okay." Mandy's words were slowing down, and she was having even more trouble keeping her eyes open. "I love you, Bear."

"I love you too."

Bear waited until her breathing turned rhythmic before getting to his feet and tossing another blanket on top of her. When he was sure she was asleep, he slipped into the kitchen. Rosie was enjoying a fresh cup of coffee. She'd set out another mug for him.

"Helped myself," she said. "Hope you don't mind. Just couldn't get warm."

"Good thinking." Bear poured himself a cup and sipped on it. He didn't care if he burnt his tongue. The warmth seeping into his body was well worth the pain. "Thanks." He waited until she met his eyes. "For everything."

"Of course." She tapped her phone. "Jenny's going to be okay. She's warming up. Fell asleep almost instantly."

"Mandy's out too." Bear poked his head back into the living room just to make sure, then sat down next to Rosie. "I'm sure they had some choice words."

"They're angry, yeah. They didn't need Jenny to tell them it was Mandy's idea." She shrugged. "But I think they're just happy their kid is safe. That might all change by morning."

"Fair enough."

"Bear, I have to ask." Rosie hesitated, but she met his eyes again. "What were you doing outside the deli? Are you, are you following me?"

Bear sighed. He knew how it looked. "Not for the reason you think."

"Okay." She tucked a piece of hair behind her ear. She wasn't running, so that was a good sign. "What's the reason?"

"You've been acting strange ever since that night we heard the Seneca Guns."

"This again?" She shook her head. "I told you, I don't like loud noises."

"I think it's more than that. Jed told me about the meeting at the deli. Something else is going on."

Rosie sat back in her chair and sipped her coffee. She was silent for so long, Bear wasn't sure she'd ever answer. Then she set down the mug and looked him straight in his face. "Reed was murdered."

Bear remembered this. "You said they never found out who did it."

"But did I say that I was there?"

"What happened?"

Rosie leapt up, like she was going to leave and never come back. She started pacing instead. "He was shot. Once in the chest. I didn't see it, but I heard it. I saw him after. It was so loud. The gunshot sounded like a canon. Like a hundred canons going off at once. When I heard that sound the other night, I panicked."

"Have you ever seen anyone about that?" Bear asked. "PTSD, I mean?"

Rosie shook her head. "Talked to a therapist a couple times. My sister wanted me to. But it wasn't helping. I needed to find my own way to deal with it."

"And what way was that?"

"The shop. Put everything I had into that." She shook her head. They both knew what kind of trouble that had brought her. "Spent more time with my sister and her kids. I have a niece and a nephew. They're perfect. Take after me more than her, I think."

"I know from experience that avoiding those thoughts doesn't make them go away." Bear held up a hand. "I'm not telling you to go see a therapist. God knows I'm not good at following their advice either. I'm just saying, it's hard for me to believe you let this go. If they never found out who killed him, you'd want answers."

Rosie stopped pacing and sat back down, drumming her fingers on the table. "I've tried. Couldn't find anything. Not anything important anyway. Not yet."

"The meeting at the deli," Bear said. "That has something to do with it, doesn't it?"

"Why are you so obsessed with that?" Rosie's voice wasn't harsh, but it was guarded.

"Because I think you know more than you're willing to tell me. Maybe you don't trust me. That's fair." He held up his hand again when it looked like she wanted to protest. "But the Murrays getting harassed? The road being blown up? And now this sub that Mandy found? That wasn't a pleasure boat, Rosie. Had to be something else."

"Like what?"

Bear shrugged. "I'd need pictures to be sure." He wasn't going to let her change topics again. "Tell me about the meeting. I already know about the resistance group."

"How?"

"Jed and I had a talk earlier in the evening."

"Did your fists do most of the talking?"

Bear looked down at his hands. "Might've. But at the end of our *conversation*, we realized we want the same thing."

"Which is?"

"To keep the people we care about safe." Bear decided to go for broke. "Did you or anyone else at that meeting set the bomb?"

Rosie looked taken aback. It took her a few seconds to find her voice again. "No. God, no."

"Then who did it?"

"Rocky Pointe Reality." She leaned forward. Her gaze bore into him. "They're behind everything."

"Why?" He couldn't wrap his head around it. "Property values will go down. People will leave. Why would they want that?"

"We think the company is a front for something else." Rosie sat back now, looking exhausted by the admission. "That's why they're buying up all these properties. They want it for something else."

"Like what?"

"I don't know. That's the truth."

Bear decided to let that go. "Alright. Well, what do you know about Ethan Gray?"

"Not much. I know he's one of the main agents around here. He's pushy, but he's never gotten physical."

"You know where he lives?"

"Avon," Rosie said. "Road won't be fixed for a while."

Like that was going to stop Bear. "I'll find a way."

25

BEAR HAD CONVINCED THE PICKETTS TO LET HIM BORROW THEIR BOAT TO do a little reconnaissance, despite their still smoldering anger. They all wanted to know what the girls had found. Bear believed everything Mandy had told him—she had no reason to lie at this point. He just needed to see it for himself.

The weather had cleared overnight. A few fluffy clouds that looked like they had been painted into the sky. The sun shone bright and warm enough that Bear could get away with a light jacket.

He found himself in the middle of the sound, driving in circles around Mandy's phone. It was dead and gone by this point, but Bear could approximate the area.

It lay a good ten feet deep down there. There was no way he'd be able to see the submersible, either.

Not that he had expected to find anything.

What Mandy had described last night sounded a lot like a narco-sub used to transport cargo from South America to the States. He needed to see those pictures she took. That's the only way he'd know for sure.

If he confirmed his suspicions, what would happen next? He'd gotten hints from Rosie that Rocky Pointe Realty was buying up as much property as they could. Maybe they just wanted to corner the market. Or maybe they wanted all that property for something else.

Not for the first time, Bear's thoughts turned to Rosie and everything she'd shared with him last night. The way Reed had died—the way she had been the one to find him—sat heavy with him. He'd known plenty of people who'd met a similar end. He knew what it felt like to not know why something so terrible could happen to someone you loved. He'd fought through armies to enact his revenge, so he couldn't blame Rosie for joining a resistance group.

But to what end? If Rocky Pointe Realty drove prices down, what else were they willing to do? How far would they go to get what they wanted? If he kept sticking his neck out for people, he'd have a target on his back. That is, if he didn't already.

Bear felt like he was standing on a cliff's edge. Every moment since he'd arrived in the Outer Banks had pushed him closer to the precipice. Meeting Ethan Gray at the Murrays' house. Meeting Doyle at the ice cream shop. Then making a fool out of him back outside the Murrays. Even fighting Jed and breaking up the deli shop meeting had inched him closer.

Now it was his turn to decide whether he should step back or throw himself over the edge.

He wanted to pack up Mandy and take off tonight. She'd probably be happy about it. Where would they go then? They'd only been here for a few months. He liked the people. The view. The idea of being on the ocean, away from everything in the mainland.

Bear didn't want to give up so easily. He was tired of running. Tired of looking over his shoulder for the next threat.

His mind had already been made up when he'd started digging for answers—taking Doyle's license and going off to question Ethan Gray. Whoever was in control knew who Bear was by now. And damned if he was going to let them drive him from a place that held memories of a better time in his life.

Whipping the boat around, he headed toward Avon. He had told the Picketts he planned on doing some reconnaissance, and that was still true. Bear could use the Sound to drive right up the coast and onto Ethan Gray's front step.

Bear remembered how to get to the Rocky Pointe building, but now he was on foot and needed to stay out of sight. Waltzing into the realty office like he owned the place wouldn't work a second time. Everyone would be on the lookout for him. It was better to hang back and observe.

The afternoon was spent sitting in a café, nursing a coffee and eating a croissant. From there, he could see people filtering in and out of the real estate building. Gray never showed up. Maybe it was his day off.

One good thing came from lurking most of the day—around noon, three construction workers came in to grab coffee and a couple sandwiches. No fewer than four people came up to them to ask how long it would take to get power back and open the road. Bear overheard them saying it'd take another day or two for the power, at least a week or more for the road. The workers left soon after, probably to eat their meal in peace.

Bear had already promised himself he wouldn't walk away, but he'd feel much better once the road was open again. Just in case.

No sooner had the doorbell chimed from the construction workers leaving than Ethan Gray strolled out of his office in a three-piece navy suit, holding a leather briefcase. Bear bussed his tableware then hurried out after the man, wondering how he'd keep up without a vehicle.

Luckily for him, Gray wasn't in a hurry. And he wasn't paranoid. Bear followed him undetected to the other side of town to a diner. From across the street, he could see the agent sitting with another man at a booth. Bear was too far to read their lips, but based on their body language, the pair didn't like one another.

Less than ten minutes later, Ethan left with a scowl on his face. Bear had no idea who the other man was, but his instincts told him to stick with Gray. Sure enough, the man walked back across town and straight into a bar.

Bear didn't hesitate. He gave the man a sixty-second head start before pushing his way inside.

26

BEAR WASN'T THERE FOR SUBTLETY.

He walked through the doors of a bar called High Noon and spotted Gray on a stool across the room. The bartender had just passed him his bottle of beer, and the man had raised it to his lips for his first swig. Though he looked relieved to finally have a cold one in his hand, it would take more than just one to wash away his encounter in that diner.

Bear sat next to Gray, catching the bartender's attention. "Whatever he's having. And put his on my tab, too."

Gray did a double take of Bear, then shook his head. None of the man's previous bravado was anywhere to be seen. He looked angry. And tired. "Thanks, but no thanks. Not in the mood today, man."

"Not here to fight." Bear nodded his head at the bartender delivering his beer, then handed over his card. "Just want to chat. Something tells me this goes higher than you. And if that's the case, I'm curious about who signs the checks. I'd be more than happy to leave your name out of it."

"Just like that?" Gray looked skeptical. "No strings attached?"

"I'd ask you to leave the Murrays alone. And Rosie."

Gray scoffed. "How is Rosie, by the way? You have any meaningful conversations with her yet?"

The other guy was lashing out, trying to get under Bear's skin. "A few. She's the one who pointed me in your direction. Said you might know what happened out on the highway."

A few heads swiveled in their direction. Gray glared at Bear. "I don't know what you're talking about." He sighed. "Look, it's been a long day. Month? Year?" He laughed, but it was bitter. "I just want to have a beer in peace."

Bear flagged the bartender down. "Another round, please." He turned back to Gray. "How about two beers, a quick conversation, and a promise to not cause you anymore trouble?"

Gray tipped his head back like he couldn't believe he was considering entertaining Bear's offer. When the beers came, he grabbed his new one, slid off the stool, and slid into one of the booths in the back. Bear slid in across from the other man.

"I'm going to level with you," Bear started. "I've got it on good authority that you're behind what's going on around Hatteras. Bullying people out of their homes, forcing business owners to pay off guys so their shops don't get vandalized. Buying property and not reselling any of it. Did you blow up the road to drive prices even lower? Was it a warning to whoever's left not to fight back?"

"Are you listening to yourself?" Gray hissed, leaning closer. "How does any of that make sense? Why would I blow up the only road back to the mainland?"

"You live in Avon. Your building is in Avon."

"And I do plenty of work in Hatteras, which you so obviously pointed out."

"It's a good way to drop values," Bear repeated. "To drive people out."

"And why would I want that kind of heat? I'm already public enemy number one over there. People see me coming and they don't even answer their doors anymore."

"Is that why you send your goons doorstep to doorstep? Force people to deal with you instead of them?"

"Goons?" Gray sat back, his brows pinched together. "What are you talking about?"

"Doyle and his gang. Did you tell him to push Joseph Murray around?" Bear felt his blood boiling. "Who are you gonna sic him on next?"

Gray was silent for a beat, as though absorbing what Bear was saying. "Doyle doesn't work for me."

"Bullshit."

Gray shook his head, then grabbed his shirt with one hand and pulled it up, revealing a line of purple bruises across his ribs. "If he worked for me, do you think I'd have these?"

Bear looked between the bruises and Gray's face. "Doyle did that to you?"

Gray lowered his shirt and looked around to see if anyone had noticed. "Yes."

"Why?"

"Consequences of not closing a deal that needs to be closed."

"The house the other day?" Bear asked. "The pretentious one?"

"No." Gray waved his hand in the air between them. "That was an easy sell. A side project." Bear opened his mouth, but Gray held up a hand. "I'm not going to tell you what deal. Whatever you can do to me, they'll do ten times worse. Something tells me you still have a conscience."

"That's a dangerous assumption." Bear leaned forward. He couldn't let it go. "Help me figure out what's going on around here."

"You want to figure out what's going on?" Gray's voice took on a sharper quality. He flung his arm out, pointing to the TV above the bar. "Open your fucking eyes."

Bear looked at the TV. It was playing a news report from earlier in the day. A man with a microphone was standing on the beach, caution tape and a group of police officers in the background. It looked like they were combing the sand for something. The headline at the bottom of the screen said a dead body had washed ashore following last night's storm. The investigation was ongoing.

Gray didn't wait for Bear to say anything else. He stood and tossed a hundred-dollar bill down on the table. "I'm outta here." He looked at

Bear like a man caught in a trap, but after a few seconds, his face steeled. "I'm not saying anything else or my kid'll end up dead." He shook his head one last time. "Good luck, man. You're gonna need it."

27

MANDY KNEW SHE HAD MESSED UP BY PLAYING HOOKY AND LYING TO BEAR and sneaking out to the submersible at night. She never should've done something so stupid without preparing better. And she never should have convinced Jenny to go along with her. They had almost died, and it was all Mandy's fault.

Why did Bear have to rub salt in the wound by having Rosie babysit her?

Sure, she got to spend the entire day in the ice cream parlor, and Rosie had said she could eat as much ice cream as she wanted, but that was only exciting after the first two cones. After that, she started to feel sick and wanted to go home and curl up under her blankets.

She hadn't talked to Jenny since yesterday, but Rosie had told said she was okay. Her parents were furious with Mandy, and even though they had every right to be, it still hurt Mandy's feelings. She had done a really stupid thing, but it had never occurred to her that something bad could've happened to them.

That had to count for something, right?

Both of their phones were gone, and Bear made sure someone watched Mandy like a hawk every minute of every day. Not that she had any interest in running off somewhere else. She'd learned her lesson.

Now she just wanted to sleep this off until everyone forgot what she'd done.

The worst part was, she didn't know how Jenny was feeling right now. They'd been too exhausted to talk on the boat ride home, and their parents had whisked them in opposite directions as soon as they'd made land. Without a way to contact each other, Mandy had no idea if they were still friends. Best case scenario, she'd see Jenny in school on Monday. Worst case? Her parents shuttled her back to the mainland to stay with her grandma in a different school district. Mandy would never see her again.

It would've happened eventually—Mandy knew they wouldn't stay in North Carolina forever—but she hadn't expected it so soon. And if Jenny really was gone—or if she refused to talk to Mandy— then Mandy would be on her own. No one else in school liked her, and they'd like her even less if they found out what she'd done.

At that thought, Mandy slouched further in her seat. She hadn't thought about how horrible it would be if the whole school found out they'd almost drowned during the storm last night. *Great. Something else to have nightmares about tonight.*

Rosie looked up from the ice cream counter when Mandy shifted. It had been as quiet as a funeral home after closing for the last hour or so. There were no customers, and Mandy had spent the entire morning shutting down any conversation.

"Hey," Rosie said softly. "You hungry? You want some lunch?"

Mandy rolled her eyes, not even trying to hide it. "All you have here is ice cream."

"No, but we can get something down the street. Pizza? A hot dog?" Rosie's voice got brighter the more she spoke. "My treat."

"Considering I have no money, that wasn't exactly in question."

Rosie didn't let Mandy's attitude burst her bubble. "What are your favorite pizza toppings?"

"Anchovies," Mandy said.

"Oh, good. I love anchovies. Not many people do."

Mandy blanched and looked over at Rosie. She tried to hide her shocked expression, but it was too late. "You don't really like anchovies, do you?" Mandy asked.

Rosie made a face. "No way. They're gross." She laughed when Mandy sagged in relief. "Come on, what do you really want?"

"Nothing," Mandy said. She wasn't going to give in. "I'm not hungry."

At that moment, Mandy's stomach chose to growl. It was so quiet that there was no way Rosie didn't hear it. "Come on, I know you want something."

Mandy dug in her heels. "I said, I'm not hungry."

Rosie sighed and walked out from behind the counter. She sat down across from Mandy and started fiddling with the napkin holder, lining it perfectly with the edge of the table. "Is there a reason why you hate me? Did I do something wrong?"

Mandy looked away. "No."

"No, there's no reason why you hate me? Or no, I didn't do anything wrong?"

"You didn't do anything wrong."

"So, there is a reason."

Mandy looked up with a scowl. She'd tricked her again. "Maybe."

"What is it?" Rosie asked. When Mandy didn't answer right away, Rosie folded her hands in front of her. "Look, it's going to be a lot more comfortable for both of us if you just tell me. You can continue to hate me if you want, but I'll try to be less annoying. There's no reason for both of us to suffer."

She had a point there. "I don't hate you," Mandy said. "It's just hard."

"What is?"

"Seeing the way my dad looks at you." Mandy hadn't meant to be that honest. The words had tumbled out of her mouth before she could shove them back inside. Now that they were out, there was no denying them. "I can tell he likes you."

"And that's a bad thing?" Rosie asked. "Because I like him too."

Mandy blinked away the tears that were forming in the corners of her eyes. It was a lot easier to be mad at someone than to talk about your feelings. "I just don't like it, okay? It's too soon."

"Too soon?" Rosie's brow pinched together. "We've known each other a couple of months. Actually, we've known each other for a couple of decades if you want to be technical about it." She frowned when she saw her joke didn't land. "It's not like we're trying to get married. He hasn't even tried to kiss me."

"He's not ready. Not yet."

Rosie leaned closer. "Why? What do you mean?"

A tear spilled down Mandy's cheek. She didn't want to talk about this, but she couldn't stop the flood of emotion. "He still misses Sasha. And so do I. That's why he hasn't kissed you. And that's why I don't want you two to get together."

Rosie sat back in her chair. She took a moment to answer. "Who's Sasha?"

"He was in love with her. She was perfect." Mandy didn't want to hurt Rosie's feelings, but there was no way the woman could under-stand what she was feeling. "And someone killed her. Just like that. One minute she was there, and the next she was gone forever." Mandy didn't bother holding back the tears now. "And we never talk about it. But I know it hurts him because it hurts me, too. And I miss her so much." She wasn't sure she was even making sense anymore. "I had a picture of her in my backpack, and it's gone now. It's in the Sound, and I'll never get that back. And I'm so afraid that I'm going to forget what she looks like. That Bear will forget her too. And I don't want that to happen. I don't want to forget."

Rosie tried to lay a hand on Mandy's arm, but Mandy shrugged it off. A few seconds later, Rosie spoke, her voice trembling with emotion. "I know what it feels like to lose someone you love. My brother was murdered. And even though it's been a couple of years, it still hurts. Sometimes I worry that I'm forgetting him, too." She took a deep breath. "I have lots of pictures of him, but what about his laugh? Do I remember what that sounded like? Or the way he'd say hello when he answered the phone. Or how he used to yell my name when he'd get mad at me when we were kids? It's weird the things you latch onto when you realize that person isn't going to be around anymore."

Mandy wiped at her tears with the sleeve of her sweatshirt, simply replaced with the next ones. She didn't know what to say. Nothing was going to make it better for either one of them.

"I know you miss her. I know Bear does, too. And I bet you both wish she was here instead of me." There was no pain in her voice. Just fact. "I wish Reed was still here. I'd do anything to get him back. Anything to make sure he didn't die in vain."

Mandy looked up at the fierceness in Rosie's voice. The woman wore a look of pure determination. Her usually kind eyes were full of anger. And not for the first time, Mandy felt like she knew a lot more than she was letting on.

"The last thing I want to do is make you feel like I'm replacing Sasha," Rosie said. "Because I'm not. I never could. And I don't want to. I like your dad. He's a good man and he makes me feel safe. But who knows if anything will happen between us? Life is crazy right now. We might've already missed our chance. Besides, we're still getting to know each other. Maybe he'll find something he doesn't like. And then you won't even have to worry about me."

Mandy wanted to ask what she meant by that, but Rosie was already getting to her feet.

"Come on," Rosie said. "I'm starving. Let's go get that pizza."

28

Bear didn't bother sticking around Avon after Ethan Gray walked out of High Noon. He didn't want to cause more trouble for Gray and his family

It didn't sit right with him.

Rosie had said Rocky Pointe Realty was behind all of this, that Ethan Gray and his people had blown up the highway. Gray was afraid of something—or someone—and wasn't willing to risk getting caught talking to Bear. With the sub and the dead body in the mix, all of this seemed to be much bigger than Bear had thought.

He wasn't going to get more information in Avon, at least not right now. Without waiting any longer, Bear drove back to Buxton, docked the boat, and returned to the Picketts' house to hand over the keys. Gordon answered the door. He looked tired. And he didn't invite Bear inside.

"Did you find anything?" the man asked.

"No." Bear didn't miss the way Gordon's face fell. "It was always a long shot. The water is deep enough that it's hard to see to the bottom on a good day, and the mud's still kicked up from the storm."

Gordon nodded his head. "You have any idea what that was? Why it washed up shore before the storm?"

"I don't think it did wash up onto the shore. I think someone stashed it there."

Gordon's eyebrows pinched together. "You mean someone drove that thing here and hid it?"

Bear nodded. "The way Mandy had described it, sounds like the kind of sub drug traffickers use to transport their product. Coast Guard's been having a lot of trouble with them. The tech is getting a lot more sophisticated."

"Jesus. Drug traffickers, really?"

"Ever have any trouble with that around here?" Bear asked.

"I don't know. Probably. Never really paid much attention to it." Gordon looked beyond him, out toward the sea. "I mean, you hear of people getting arrested, but almost never anyone around here. Most of them are farther north. At least those are the ones that get caught."

"Let me ask you something else," Bear started. There was no easy way to transition to the topic. "How well do you know Rosie?"

Gordon's gaze landed back on Bear's face. "Does this have something to do with her brother?"

"Why would you say that?"

"He was mixed up in all that. Drugs, I mean. That's how he died."

"I thought he was shot."

"He was." Gordon rubbed at the back of his neck. "Look, I don't want to speak out of turn here."

"Rosie already told me some of it. That she was there. That she found him."

The other man nodded. "Reed dealt drugs. The cops raided his house when Rosie was there. She was in the back room, I guess. Didn't see the how the whole thing went down. According to the cops, Reed tried to go for a weapon. They shot him in self-defense."

"The cops shot him?" Bear asked. That wasn't how Rosie had made it sound.

Gordon nodded. "Rosie swore up and down that he'd never do that, but they found the gun. And he had the drugs. That part she couldn't deny."

"She knew? About him selling?"

"Not sure, but everyone pretty much knew he was an addict. I think that's why Rosie was over there. He was trying to get clean. Pretty tragic timing."

"Yeah." There was a beat of silence. "How was Rosie after that?"

"That sort of thing changes a person, you know?" Gordon shrugged. "Marissa used to be a lot closer to her. They grew up together. I'm from the mainland." He smirked like this was an inside joke between him and his wife, but the sadness didn't leave his eyes. "After Reed died, they drifted apart. Rosie pretty much kept to herself. Opened the ice cream shop. We tried to include her in stuff. Invited her everywhere. But when someone never accepts your invitations, you stop going out of your way to include them, you know?"

"Is there anyone she does hang out with regularly?" When Gordon gave him a suspicious look, Bear held up his hands. "This isn't some jealous lover type shit, in case you're wondering. I just think she might be mixed up is something bad."

"Well, there was Jed. Everyone agreed that was a mistake. He's intense, but he'd never hurt her. And I think he's gotten the message at this point. He tries to make a move every once in a while, but she shuts it down and he walks away with his tail between his legs."

Bear had to search his memory for the name of the neighbor he met a few days ago. "What about Zeke? He a good guy?"

"Oh yeah. He and his wife do a lot for the community. Lots of volunteer work. Make sure everyone's happy and taken care of. Everyone wants him to run for council, but he's not interested. Good for the other team because he'd win by a landslide."

"You know anything about a meeting in the deli every Friday night?"

"No, can't say that I do. What's the meeting for?"

Bear dodged the other man's question. "She doing okay?"

"Much better now. Temperature is all back to normal. A couple bruises, but they'll fade." Gordon's eyes were still sad. "She's been having nightmares. Don't think she's gonna go out in the ocean any time soon."

"I think the same goes for Mandy. She learned a hard lesson yesterday." Bear let the silence stretch between them for a moment or two. "Listen, I know you're still upset at her. And trust me, I get it. She did a stupid thing. But I think it might be good for the girls to see each other. I know Mandy would like to apologize. To Jenny and to both of you."

"I appreciate that," Gordon said. He looked like he meant it, but his mouth was set in a firm line. "But it's going to take some time. I think right now, Jenny just needs some space."

Bear nodded and held out his hand. "Thanks for letting me borrow the boat. If you need anything, you have my number."

Gordon shook Bear's hand. He looked appreciative, but still guarded. "Stay safe out there."

As Bear turned to leave, he wondered if that was even possible at this point. Something told him he was way in over his head already, and if he wasn't careful, he'd be the next one swept out to sea.

29

BEAR HAD ONE MORE STOP TO MAKE BEFORE PICKING UP MANDY FROM THE ice cream shop. He'd already been contemplating paying a visit to the reporter. After his conversation with Gordon about Reed, Bear wanted to know more. Newspapers weren't innocent from slanting the truth in favor of a juicy story, but they were a lot more willing to print the facts that no one wanted to talk about. If nothing else, Bear would be able to verify Gordon's story.

The Free Island Press was headquartered in a small building in Buxton. It was comprised of one large room with a front desk and a handful of cubicles in the middle. The only other rooms with doors were the tiny kitchen, a bathroom, and the editor's office.

Bear could see all of it through the front door window. It was Saturday, but the reporter had struck him as a burning-the-midnight-oil kind of person, and sure enough, he was sitting at a computer in the middle of the room, drinking coffee and typing away on the keyboard. Bear tried the handle, but it was locked. He knocked instead.

The man looked up, surprised by the intrusion. Bear gave a friendly wave, and the reporter got up and opened the door a crack, standing in the opening with a confused look on his face. "Can I help you?"

"My name is Riley Logan." Bear stuck out his hand. "We met the other day at the site of the explosion?"

"I remember you," the man said, shaking his hand. "Ben Carroll."

"I'm not going to parse words here. I'm trying to understand what's been happening around the island lately. I thought maybe you could help me out."

Ben looked beyond Bear, first right, then left. Then he stepped to the side. "You better come in."

Bear didn't hesitate. The office was warm and smelled of coffee and cigarette smoke. He wondered if Ben liked to sneak one on the weekends, or if the nicotine had just seeped into the walls and never let go.

"I'm sorry to barge in on you like this."

Ben waved him off, leading him back toward his desk. "I was playing solitaire. Writer's block."

Sure enough, the game was up on Ben's computer. He was close to winning. "How many games have you played today?" Bear asked.

"Twenty-seven." Ben grinned. "Only lost three." Then he sobered. "You're not from here, are you?"

"What makes you say that?"

"You ask questions." Ben laughed. "And I've lived here my whole life. Don't remember seeing you much until recently."

"I visited here in the summer when I was a kid. Have my own now. Thought I'd bring her here to see what she thinks of my old stomping ground."

"And?"

"She hates it." They both laughed. "Gotta say, Hatteras isn't how I remembered it. Not sure if it's because I'm older now. Or because it's winter. Or if it's just changed."

"It's definitely changed. Outside of tourist season, you see a few more cracks, but the island's been sinking."

"Literally or metaphorically?"

"Both." Ben sighed and looked away. "This used to be a pretty tight-knit town. Lotta locals. Lately, seems like half the population is gone. Fewer tourists too."

"You have any prevailing theories?"

"Plenty." Ben grinned like he was full of secrets. "None that I'm willing to put in print."

"Any you could share off the record?"

Ben studied him for a moment. "Why are you so interested?"

Bear knew he'd have to give a little to get a little. "Some friends of mine have been getting harassed. The Murrays?" Ben nodded like he knew exactly who Bear was talking about. "And Rosie Callaway. She owns the ice cream shop."

"Yeah, I know Rosie." He sounded sad. "And what? You want to be the hero?"

"Actually, I'd rather sit back and enjoy my time here. Teach my daughter how to fish. How to appreciate the water. But there are a couple characters around town aren't letting me do that."

"Who?"

"Ethan Gray from Rocky Pointe Realty. A man named Andrew Doyle. I'm not looking to stir up any shit. I just want answers."

"If you're looking for the truth, you're bound to stir up shit." Ben chuckled. "Trust me, I know."

Bear decided to go for broke. "You said you grew up here. Did you know Rosie's brother? Reed Callaway?"

Ben stiffened. "Yeah, I knew him."

"Me too. Long time ago. We used to hang out when we were kids. When this place was bigger and brighter. We used to get into all sorts of trouble. It was a blast." Bear noticed Ben relax. "Didn't know until recently that Rosie was his sister. I was sad to hear he'd passed."

"Yeah." Ben sighed. Rubbed a hand along the back of his neck. "He was my best friend in high school. He moved away, and we stayed in touch for a while. When he came back, it was like he'd never left. For a while, at least."

"I heard he got mixed up in some drugs."

"You heard right." Ben shook his head. "He was always a wild kid, but he didn't do any of that while he was here. Not sure what happened to him when he left. Bad breakup or some hard times. You know how it goes. When he came back, he seemed like himself. But it didn't take long before everyone noticed he was drinking a little too much. Then he started hitting the harder stuff."

"Like what?"

"Coke mostly."

"Was he selling?"

"I think so, yeah. Why else would he have that much in his apartment, you know?"

"And the cops busted him for that?" Bear asked.

Ben nodded. "That was a tough night. We'd gotten into a fight that morning. I told him he had to get clean. He was pushing people away. I'd caught him passed out cold on his front step more times than I can count. Rosie was worried about him too. He'd tried rehab programs before, but none of them stuck." A look of pain crossed over his face. "The night before, he'd been drinking and driving. Got into an accident. Almost killed a seven-year-old kid and her family. He was shaken up about it. I think he would've tried harder this time. He never wanted to hurt anyone, you know? He just wanted his own pain to go away."

"You think he was going for a gun when the cops shot him?"

"I don't know. I wish I did." Ben sighed. "I didn't know him as well as I thought I did. For a while, I tried to dig deeper into the story. I wanted it to be some conspiracy or something. But the gun was there. The drugs were there. The story wrote itself."

"And what about Rosie? How did she handle it all?"

"Not well. That was her big brother, you know? She and her sister Rhoda didn't always get along. Too different. Reed was the oldest, but he played mediator a lot. Rhoda liked to ignore what was going on right in front of her. Didn't want to deal with it. She had her own problems. A family to take care of. But Rosie couldn't let it go. I mean, she was there, you know? That's going to haunt her for the rest of her days. She wanted revenge. But we couldn't find anything on the cops. At the end of the day, they were just doing their job."

"You seem to have accepted it better than Rosie," Bear said.

He shrugged. "I deal in death a lot as a journalist. I know when a story is rotten. This one was tragic, but I don't think they were out to get him."

Bear believed him. But there had to be a reason why Rosie wouldn't let it go. "What about the drugs?" Bear asked. "You find out where he got them from?"

"You'd make a good journalist."

Bear laughed. "Thanks."

"We think he was helping traffickers. Not sure if he was selling himself, but he was involved. Storing it at his place, helping them move it. Couldn't ever find any connections or contacts though."

"Hatteras have a lot of trouble with trafficking?"

"About as much as anywhere else, though I think it's gotten worse lately. Nothing in the papers, and no arrests, but you hear murmurings. You know what areas to avoid at night."

"You hear about that body that washed up overnight?" Bear had watched the entire news report at the bar after Gray had left. "Know anything else?"

"Matter of fact, I do." Ben sat back down in his chair and minimized his game of solitaire. He opened up his emails and searched until he found the right one. "Got a source that says it was a Colombian national. Name was Luis Vargas. No info on him yet, but he wasn't here on vacation, that's for sure. Body was a bit mangled when he came to shore. They think a shark got hold of him at some point. He also had a knife wound in his chest.

"Somebody dumped him," Bear offered.

"Seems like it."

"What if I told you my kid found a narco sub stashed along the highway?"

Ben snapped to attention. "I'd say I'd be interested in learning more."

"She's got pictures in the Cloud." Bear felt strange repeating the words, like he knew what that meant. "You help me trace this back to someone here on the stateside, and I'll let you use them in a story. Anonymously, of course."

"Of course."

30

BEAR FROZE IN PLACE AS SOON AS HE WALKED THROUGH THE DOOR OF Rosemary's Ice Cream Palace. Mandy jumped to her feet, a mostly eaten pizza on the table in front of her. Rosie looked up at him with such cold, detached eyes.

"Mandy, can you wait in here for a minute?" Rosie asked, coming out from behind the counter. "I'd like to talk to your dad for a minute."

"Uh, sure." Mandy said. The look she gave Bear was a mix between *I'm sorry* and *You had it coming.* "No problem."

Bear backtracked through the door and stood to the side to let Rosie out. As soon as the door shut behind them, she crossed her arms over her chest like it was armor between them. "I know about Sasha."

Bear's chest squeezed at hearing her name. Images from the last time he saw her flooded his brain. The shot. The blood. Her crumpling in the backseat of the car. He tried to replace them with happier memories. Her smile. Her laugh. Her getting annoyed at him over something, and the way her face would flush when she was angry. The way her eyes would soften when he took her hands and stepped closer. They could drive each other crazy, but it never lasted. They always came back to each other.

Or at least they used to.

"I wasn't trying to keep her a secret," Bear said. "But it's not easy for me to talk about."

"And you think talking about Reed is? I opened up to you, Bear. I told you something that haunts me every minute of every day. You relate to that feeling. And you couldn't confide in me about it. I thought you trusted me."

"I do," he said, though he felt a twinge of doubt. "And I feel for you, but it's not the same." Bear tried to keep his voice even, but there was a spark of anger there that he couldn't control. "I asked about Reed. I know how he died. I know what happened with the cops. It's not like you told me the whole truth either."

Rosie's jaw went slack at the same time she dropped her arms. "You were asking around about Reed? Fact-checking my story? What the hell, Riley?"

"Don't turn this on me," Bear said. "I've been asking you from the beginning what's going on and how you're mixed up in all this. Don't blame me for doing my due diligence."

She crossed her arms again. "Your due diligence? I don't owe you shit."

"Likewise." Bear let his words sink in. Then he took a deep breath and tried to recalibrate his feelings. "Listen, I wanted to tell you about Sasha. I wanted you to know how hard it would be for me to talk about. That I'm still in a lot of pain."

"So is Mandy." Rosie's voice was quieter, not without an edge. "Did you ever think that's why she hates me?"

"She doesn't hate you."

"Well, she sure as hell doesn't like me—"

"Trouble in paradise?" someone asked.

Bear turned and saw Doyle, strolling up to them like he was out for a late afternoon walk. "Keep moving, man. Not in the mood for you today."

"Good thing I'm not here for you, then." He turned to Rosie. "We're gonna need your next payment early. As in now."

She blanched. "I just paid your last goon yesterday. I don't have any extra money."

Doyle took a step closer. "Then you better find it."

Bear put a hand on Doyle's chest and shoved him backwards. He felt his pent-up rage rising to the surface. "Let it go, man. This is not going to end well for you. Remember last time?"

"I do. How is Old Joe doing? Heard he didn't even go to the hospital. Might have to go pay him another visit and see—"

Bear didn't let him finish the sentence. He was tired of not getting answers. Tired of chasing something that seemed to retreat further from him every time he got closer to it. Whatever was going on, Doyle knew something. Maybe on another day Bear would've tried asking nicely. But today was not that day.

Doyle didn't see the punch coming. It landed square on his jaw, snapping his head to the right. He stumbled back, still on his feet. Bear waited for his eyes to refocus before swinging again. This time, Doyle blocked it, but Bear had anticipated that. He brought up a knee and tried to get the other man between his legs, but he missed. Doyle took the opportunity to swing on Bear next, connecting with his ear. A shot of pain lanced its way through his head and down his shoulder.

Rosie was shouting behind him. "Stop! Please. Bear, you're just making it worse."

Maybe he was just making it worse. Or maybe he'd finally teach Doyle a lesson.

Bear blocked another swing and sent a punch into Doyle's gut. He heard the other man wheeze and took the opportunity to lunge at him, tackling him to the ground and sitting on his chest. A dozen jabs to the face later, Bear's knuckles were bloody, and Doyle was out cold.

The door opened and Mandy stuck her head outside. "Holy shit, Bear. You kicked his ass."

Bear glared at her. "Get back inside." He shook his head and muttered, "At least she didn't drop an F-bomb."

Mandy groaned in frustration but did as she was told. Rosie walked up to him, looking scared and frustrated. "Bear, that wasn't a good idea. Next time he comes back, he's gonna bring his friends."

"Not if I get to them first." Bear dug around in Doyle's coat pockets and pulled out his phone.

Rosie was silent as Bear held the phone up to Doyle's face to trigger the facial recognition software. As expected, the phone was empty of anything important. No pictures or text messages or browsing history. There was a slew of phone numbers. Several repeated at least a couple times a day.

"Bingo," Bear said.

He brought out his own phone and snapped pictures of the numbers.

He also scrolled through the settings to take pictures of the SIM card information. He might not know how exactly to track a phone, but he knew the information to get the job done. After that, Bear tucked the phone back into the man's coat. Then he waved at Mandy through the front door, and she stepped to his side, careful to avoid the unconscious Doyle.

"Lock up and go home," Bear told Rosie, swinging an arm around Mandy's shoulders. "And think about taking tomorrow off."

31

BEAR MADE MANDY STICK CLOSE BEHIND HIM AS HE CLEARED THEIR
house. He had measures in place to make sure no one got in without his
knowledge, but it was worth double-checking.

When Bear finished going over the house, the two sat down on the
couch, Bear's arm thrown over the back of it and Mandy's head resting
on his chest. She was still exhausted from yesterday's ordeal, and he felt
better having her within arm's reach.

He was in the middle of figuring out his next step when Mandy
raised her head and stared him down. "What?" he asked.

"Do you trust Rosemary?"

Bear didn't answer right away. He didn't expect the loaded question.
"Why?"

Mandy shrugged. "I have a weird feeling."

"A weird feeling," Bear repeated. "Care to elaborate?"

"Something just doesn't feel right."

Bear huffed out a laugh. "That's not an elaboration. You just
rephrased what you already said."

Mandy sat up straight, pushing away from him. "I don't know what
else to say. I don't trust her."

"She's gone through a lot. People are complicated. They all have their own motivations. That doesn't make them bad."

"I never said she was bad," Mandy said. "I just don't think we should trust her."

"There's no *we* here. You're not—"

"—involved. Yeah, I got that." Mandy brushed her hair off her shoulder and rolled her eyes. "Fine, then. I don't think *you* should trust her."

"But you have no reason to think that. No evidence, right?"

Mandy threw up her arms. "You listen to your gut all the time! Why won't you listen to mine?"

"Because I'm older. And wiser. Much wiser."

"And much older," Mandy grumbled.

Bear ignored the jab. His mind had been working in the background, trying to figure out who he could call to help him figure out the names behind those numbers on Doyle's phone.

That list was shorter than it had ever been. Bear wasn't about to tap into any of Noble's resources. That was a messy situation on the best of days

That also meant his options were limited. Extremely limited.

"You still talk to that kid from New York? The computer kid? What was his name?"

Mandy flushed. "You mean Marcus? Yeah, I still talk to him."

"He still into computers and stuff?"

"Yeah. His family got a huge settlement from that case with the pharmaceutical company." Mandy rushed on, as though she thought the faster she talked, the less Bear would notice her blushing. "He's bought a lot more stuff. It's pretty high tech."

"Good. Give him a call."

Mandy stilled. "What?"

"Call him up on the face thing. I wanna give him a little test."

"A test?" Mandy arched an eyebrow at him. "What kind of test?"

"Just call him, will you?" Bear liked watching Mandy squirm, but their time was also limited. He'd give her a little shit to remind her that he was in charge here, but they really did need the kid's help.

Mandy informed Bear that it was called FaceTime before she dialed his number. She angled it away from Bear while they waited, but Marcus picked up right away. If Mandy's face got any redder, she'd turn into a tomato.

"Hey, sexy," Marcus said. His voice was lower than it was last time they'd seen him, and Bear wasn't sure if he was going through puberty or if he was just trying to impress Mandy. "What's up?"

Bear grabbed Mandy's hand and turned the camera to include him in the picture. "Hey, cutie. Not much. What's up with you?"

Marcus disappeared for a second as he dropped his phone in surprise. When he came back into the picture, he couldn't look Bear in the eyes through the phone. "Mr. Logan. Sir. I-I didn't know you were there."

Bear kept his face completely emotionless, but he was howling on the inside. "Clearly."

"Sir, I-I'm so sorry."

"What are you sorry for, Marcus?"

Mandy groaned and put her face in her other hand. "Bear, please."

"I shouldn't talk to your daughter like that, sir. Or anyone's daughter. Or anyone. At all. Ever." Marcus was now brighter than Mandy. "It won't happen again, sir."

"See that it doesn't." Bear let the silence stretch on until everyone was uncomfortable. "Marcus, do you want to redeem yourself?"

The kid sat up straight. "Yes, sir. Absolutely, sir. Anything. What can I do for you?" Marcus thought for a second then added, "Sir."

"I'm sending you two images. I want you to track the numbers on them. Think you can do that?"

"Of course." The phone jostled a little bit as Marcus saw the incoming messages. He swiveled around his room until he was in front of his computer. Bear saw three monitors set up on the desk before Marcus set the phone down in a holder that kept him firmly in view. His room was a disaster. "This'll just take a second."

Bear let Marcus do his thing. The kid was efficient. Despite his overly familiar greeting with Mandy, Bear liked him. He had been a good friend to Mandy, and she didn't make many of those. It reminded

Bear of her situation with Jenny. Mandy still felt bad about what had happened, but some friends weren't meant to be forever.

"Okay, I'm seeing five different numbers on here," Marcus said, interrupting Bear's thoughts.

"Any 252 numbers? They'd be local."

"Three of them, yeah." Marcus hit a few keystrokes on his computer. "Outer Banks, huh?" He looked at the camera with a smile. "My parents and I go there every summer. It's pretty cool."

"Yeah, it's awesome," Mandy said. Bear caught her eye, and she shrugged. "It's just boring in the winter."

Marcus brightened. "Will you be there this summer?"

Bear interjected. "Not sure yet. Depends on how this all plays out." Bear let his own voice deepen, and he was glad to see it had the desired effect. "But you're not going to tell anyone we're here, are you Marcus?"

Terror filled the kid's eyes. "N-no, sir. No one."

"Good." Bear waited for the kid to go on, only to find silence on the other end. "The numbers, Marcus."

"Right. Right." Marcus hit a few more keystrokes, clicked around, and his face lit up again. "Okay, three local numbers. One is a cell phone registered to a man named Clint Michaels. Second one is a landline that belongs to Terry Matthews."

"What about the third number?" Bear asked.

Marcus' brows furrowed. He clicked around a few times, growing agitated. "I'm not sure. It's pinging around all over the place, going through a bunch of different locations. This'll take me a while."

"Send me what you have on the others. Picture and background info. Criminal records. Home addresses if you can find them. Keep working on the other number and the ones from out of state. When you find something, text me directly."

"I can do that." Marcus looked excited now, less distracted by the fear Bear had earlier instilled in him. "Anything else?"

"Yeah." Bear had to stop himself from smirking. "Come up with a couple dozen other ways to answer the phone when my daughter calls you."

Bear stayed on the phone long enough to see Marcus' eyes go wide before he ended the call.

32

When they returned home, Bear gave Mandy his spare phone and instructed her to go over to the Murray's and sit tight. It would serve a dual purpose in that they could keep an eye on each other. Mandy was not better off left to her own devices, and although Joseph Murray had once been a capable soldier—having served in Viet Nam—he was well past his prime. And still recovering from those nasty bruises from Doyle. But they were out, so she got to stay home by herself for the time being.

The only person Bear didn't have eyes on was Rosie. He'd walked her home after their run-in with Doyle, leaving him on the sidewalk. Bear was sure he hadn't seen the last of him. He hoped the altercation had allowed him time to gather some intelligence before they met again.

Doyle and his goons likely knew where Rosie lived, but she'd refused to come back to Bear's house or stay with the Murrays. She'd mentioned that her sister lived farther south in Ocracoke, so Bear hoped Rosie would at least go stay with her. He was the one pissing everyone off, but at this point, Doyle knew he could get to Bear through Rosie. Although Rosie and her business were useful to them.

But how long would that last?

That was why Bear had decided to go on the offensive. He wasn't ready to kick the hornet's nest, but he still wanted to give it a poke. Bear shook his head. He was in a desperate position if some fourteen-year-old kid was his best chance at figuring out what the hell was happening on Hatteras.

The kid was good at what he did. He'd either end up in the CIA or in jail. There wasn't a whole of in between for people with his skills. Bear couldn't imagine sitting behind a computer all day, but that was just him.

Mandy was on standby to relay information. She'd know what information was most relevant to Bear while Marcus worked on tracking down those other numbers. In the meantime, he'd followed the address attached to the landline and found himself parked outside a beach house on the canal. It'd be a good place for fishing. It was also prime real estate for anyone buying up houses on the water.

Bear was starting to get a good picture of what was going on, but he needed to fill in a few blank spaces. Hopefully this stop would prove useful.

Taking his time to get out of his truck, Bear walked up the front steps of the house. He kept his head on a swivel, watching for anyone who didn't belong. Buxton was a ghost town at this point in the year, though it was a nice enough day that the locals were enjoying the sunshine.

Floorboards creaked inside when he knocked on the door. The person on the other side paused as if looking through the peephole. A few seconds later, a lock turned and the door opened. The man looked to be in his forties with sandy blond hair that was graying at the temples. He angled his body in a way that diminished his wide shoulders. The way he stared at Bear made him think the guy could hold his own in a fight.

"Can I help you?" he asked. There was slight Southern twang to his voice.

"Terry Matthews?"

"Yes." The man's eyes narrowed ever so slightly. "Who are you?"

"Name's Riley." Bear stretched out his hand. Terry didn't hesitate.

"This is gonna sound strange, but a friend of mine is missing. All we found is his phone, and he had this number in there a few times. I was wondering if you might know where he is. Andrew Doyle?"

Terry's eyebrows pinched together. "Doyle, you said? I'm sorry, but he's no friend of mine." He stepped back, like he wanted to close the door in Bear's face. "I don't want any trouble."

"Whoa, whoa." Bear held up his hands. "I'm not here to cause any." Bear looked beyond the man, into the living room, where he saw a nice furniture set in matching blues and browns. They looked new. And expensive. "Look, if I'm being honest, Doyle isn't as much of a friend as he is an acquaintance. I think we got off on the wrong foot a few times. He's got all the subtlety of a sledgehammer."

"You're telling me."

Bear weighed his options. He might be able to force some information out of the guy. He looked scared enough. But Bear also didn't want to cause problems where there weren't any. "I'm trying to find him. He's been harassing my neighbors. I'd like to talk to him. Let him know that's not such a good idea."

"I wish I could help you. Believe me, I do." Terry looked a little more relaxed now. "He's been on my case too. Won't leave me alone, no matter how much I tell him I'm not interested in selling the house."

"He's trying to get you to sell, too, huh?" Bear wasn't exactly surprised. It fit the pattern. "What's he been doing?"

"Oh, you know, the usual. Blasting music. Ringing the doorbell at all hours of the night. Parking cars in the driveway. And that's just been the last week or so."

"You ever get a real estate agent around here? Ethan Gray?"

"This all started with him," Terry said. "He offered me some money. Not nearly what the house is worth. I've put in a lot of work over the last two years and it wasn't cheap, you know? I didn't want to sell it to begin with, and I sure as hell wasn't going to let someone lowball me on it."

"Fair enough." Bear chuckled to keep the tone light. "You see Doyle lately?"

"Not for a day or two. Thought that was gonna be him at the door. Was afraid you were one of his friends."

"You have any idea where Doyle likes to hang out? Where he goes when he's not shaking people down?"

"Wish I knew," Terry said. "Thought about calling the police, but I don't really have anything to go on. And everyone else is too scared to rock the boat."

"That might be changing." Bear held out his hand again. "Thanks for your time."

"No problem." Terry shook Bear's hand, looking him in the eyes. "If the others are ready to speak out, you point me in their direction, and I'll be there in a heartbeat."

Bear tipped his head, then backtracked down the stairs to his truck. He tried not to think of his first stop as a bust. It just proved that some of the residents around here weren't willing to be pushed around. How long would that last? Terry looked like he had money, and even he seemed to be at the end of his rope. It wouldn't be long before whoever was buying up the houses would make him an offer he couldn't refuse.

Bear pulled out of Terry's driveway and spent the next ten minutes driving around town, waiting for a plan to formulate in his mind. Before he could get anything useful together, a message came through from Mandy.

Marcus cloned Doyle's phone with that info you got off of it. He got a text from Clint Michaels telling him to meet in a motel room. Sending the address now.

Bear didn't bother texting back. He swung his truck around and headed in the opposite direction. He knew where the motel was—it was a rundown little shithole perfect for college kids and the town's seedier citizens. If Bear could get there quick enough, he'd be able to take out Clint and wait for Doyle. Offense was the best defense, after all.

Bear made it in less than fifteen minutes. He found the right motel room and knocked on the door, covering the peephole with his finger. Hearing no voices inside, he figured he'd beaten Doyle there. He'd catch Clint completely unaware.

When the door opened, Bear found himself staring down the barrel of a gun, a shit-eating grin on Clint's face. Doyle stepped out of the bathroom with a matching expression. It wasn't until two men stepped out of the room to his left and two more out of the one on his right that he knew he was fucked.

He didn't see which one hit him over the head, knocking him unconscious.

33

BEAR CAME TO JUST AS SOMEONE WAS TIGHTENING THE KNOTS ON THE rope binding his arms behind his back. He was strapped to the motel desk chair, and they'd been smart enough to strap his legs down too. He tried ripping his hands free, but the knots held. Doyle laughed in response.

Bear turned toward the noise. The room was pretty standard for a motel in this part of town. A relic of the eighties with pastel florals and tacky wallpaper. The carpet looked grimy and the fixtures ancient. You got what you paid for, but most of the people staying here didn't care.

Clint Michaels emerged from behind Bear once he'd finished tying the knot, walking to stand by Doyle. Bear didn't recognize the four other men. Two were bald with beards. They looked related. The third was a bit older with more than a few extra pounds. The last was wide-eyed and young, like maybe this was his first day on the job.

Then there was Doyle, smug as ever.

"Don't bother yelling. No one around who'll save you."

"Not too worried about it," Bear said. "Beat your ass twice before. Been looking forward to round three."

Doyle scowled. He still wore remnants of their last encounter. "Don't know if you noticed, but you're not getting the jump on me today."

Bear tipped his head back and howled with laugher. He wished he had a free hand to wipe the tears out of his eyes. "Get the jump on you? Come on, man. I know you're trying to act tough in front of your boys, but we both know those were both fair fights." Bear swiveled his head back and forth to look at the other men. "And now you had to get five of your friends to help you tie me to a chair."

Doyle reared back and drove his fist into the side of Bear's head. Bear had just enough time to angle his face away to minimize the damage, but it still hurt. He felt the bruise already blossoming under his skin, and his ear was ringing.

"Tell us what you know, and I promise I'll kill you quickly."

"You gotta be a little more specific there." Bear turned to the young kid. "Honestly, I don't think you should be getting on the job training from this guy. He doesn't know—"

Bear never got to finish his sentence. Doyle swung on him again, landing the punch in the exact same place. Bear's vision went black for a second, and he had to shake his head to clear the stars. Might not be smart to antagonize your captors when you were outnumbered six to one, but Bear didn't always fight with his head.

"Who are you?"

"Name's Riley. You can call me Mr. Logan."

"I know your name," Doyle spat. "Did a background check on you. Nothing came up. Seems suspicious."

"Not suspicious at all." Bear didn't show his relief at hearing his record was still squeaky clean. He wasn't going to give any of them anything useful. "I'm just a fine, upstanding citizen. A proud patriot. A do-gooder."

"Do-gooders get themselves killed."

"Maybe so, but we do good anyway." He turned and glared at the kid, who was starting to get uncomfortable at the attention. "It's our calling."

Doyle socked him in the face again. Bear was starting to go numb, but he knew if the man kept hitting him in the same place, he was going to draw blood soon. Or worse—break bones. "What else do you want to know?"

"Why are you sticking your nose where it don't belong?"

"I told you. I'm a do-gooder."

"With a death wish?"

Bear shrugged. "The risk makes it interesting."

"You fucking Rosie? That why you're so interested in what's going on?"

Bear stopped himself from tensing at the sound of her name. The last thing he wanted was to send more heat in her direction. "No, sir. She's a lot smarter than me. Keeps telling me to stay out of it. But I can't help myself."

"And the Murrays? How do you know them?"

"They're my next-door neighbors." Bear looked around at the other guys like, *Is he always this stupid?* "Because they live next door."

Doyle motioned to Clint, who stepped forward and landed a couple blows to Bear's gut. This was preferable to the face because he could tense his muscles and absorb most of the impact. Would probably leave bruises where Clint's knuckles found the rib bones.

Bear waited until Clint stepped back before laughing. He locked eyes with Doyle. "Getting tired, Andy? You gotta start working out if you want to be intimidating. Untie my hands, let me show you a few things."

Doyle looked like he wanted nothing more than to go toe to toe with Bear, but the chances of Bear coming out on top were high given their last encounters. Bear saw the switch in the other man's eyes when he decided it wouldn't be worth it.

"I think I'll pass. You're not going to tell me anything useful, are you?"

Bear grinned. "Nope."

"Thought so." Doyle turned to Clint. "Do whatever you want with him. Make it hurt."

"Where're you going?" Clint asked.

"I got shit to do." Doyle walked past Bear and opened the door. "Is Mandy at your house? Or did you leave her with the Murrays again?" He didn't wait for Bear to answer. "Doesn't matter. I'll find her."

Bear saw red as soon as he heard the door click closed behind him.

Clint stepped forward and whipped out a knife and held it out so the light would glint off of it into Bear's eyes. "Any last words?" he asked.

Bear didn't bother answering. All he could think about was getting to Mandy before Doyle. Without hesitation, Bear pushed off from the ground and leaned to the side. When he crashed to the ground, his weight splintered the ancient chair, giving him enough room to slip free of his bonds.

It all happened so fast, the five guys in the room didn't have time to react before Bear was on his feet, squaring off with all of them.

"You're not going to win this one," Clint said, brandishing his knife.

Bear gritted his teeth. "Watch me."

Clint moved first, but Bear used the man's momentum to send him flying across the room, headfirst into the door. It wouldn't stop him for long but Bear only needed a few seconds to lift his left foot and Sparta-kick the fat man in the stomach hard enough that he vomited down the front of his shirt and teetered backwards, falling on his ass on top of the two bald guys.

Bear returned his attention to Clint, who had recovered and was charging a second time. Only he had learned his lesson, stopping just shy of Bear's reach and slashing the knife toward Bear's chest. Bear had just enough room to jump back and roll backwards over the bed, landing on the other side and putting some distance between him and his three adversaries.

Brother One came around the side of the bed, thinking Bear was trapped against the wall. When the baldheaded man got close enough, Bear ripped the table lamp from the nightstand and smashed it over the man's head. It shattered, and Bear could already see blood beading along the top of the man's skull.

When Brother One attempted to get to his feet, Bear dragged the drawer free from the nightstand and brought it down on top of the guy's head, Bible and all. That splintered too, and this time, the man stayed still.

Brother Two howled in anger and agony, leaping over the bed to land on top of Bear. They stumbled and the wall cracked from their combined weight. As Brother Two tried to reposition to hit Bear, he tripped over his brother's body and lost his balance. Bear took advantage of the opportunity and shoved the man as hard as he would go, sending him head-first into the corner of the desk and knocking him unconscious. A bead of blood trickled from his temple.

That left Clint, who didn't wait for Bear to recover before picking up the heavy motel telephone from the other nightstand and yanking it from the wall, throwing it at Bear's head. Bear had just enough time to throw up an arm to block it, but the hard plastic hit bone and elicited a growl from his throat.

Clint was already on the move by the time Bear lowered his arm. With the knife still in one hand, Clint slashed at Bear's forearm, cutting deep and drawing blood.

The problem with people who'd rather fight with a knife was they were useless once you took away their weapon.

Bear feigned exhaustion and let his left arm drop, baiting Clint. As the other man brought the knife down to stick it in Bear's shoulder, Bear shoved the man's arm away. As Clint stumbled, Bear grasped his wrist and twisted it, knocking the knife from the man's hand. Then he pulled Clint's arm back and up, feeling the joint separating from its socket.

Clint howled in pain, but Bear didn't let up until the other man was on his knees, begging for him to stop. Bear only complied long enough to bring a boot down across the back of the man's neck, sending him face-first into the carpet.

The last adversary still on their feet was the fat man who'd been knocked down first. Even the kid was smart enough to stay out of the way.

Bear scooped up the knife from the floor and brandished it at the man. "You really wanna see who'll win this one, big guy?"

The man held up his hands and shook his head, backing up until he was on the other side of the room. Bear looked down at the kid, cowering in the corner behind a chair. He was mumbling something under his breath that sounded a lot like, "Please don't hurt me."

Bear shook his head. "Find a new career path, kid."

Then he pocketed the knife and flung open the door, making sure the coast was clear before running back to his truck with what little energy he had left. How much time had passed since Doyle left? Ten minutes? Fifteen? Mandy was smart. She'd be able to stay alive for that long. Bear didn't want to think of the alternative.

He was determined to make this his last run-in with Doyle.

34

MANDY HAD CALLED MARCUS BACK THE SECOND BEAR PULLED OUT OF THE driveway. She'd tried to play it cool, but she was so embarrassed that Marcus had answered the phone that way. Now Bear would keep a closer eye on her. She wouldn't have thought that was possible.

"Why?" she groaned into the phone as soon as Marcus had answered.

"I don't know!" His voice was higher pitched now. "I was just trying to be funny and cute!"

Mandy groaned again. "What's the number one rule?" Mandy didn't even let him answer. *"Always make sure the parents aren't eavesdropping."*

Marcus' face fell. He knew it was his fault. "I was just excited to hear from you. We haven't talked in so long."

"I know." Now it was Mandy's turn to feel guilty. "I've just been busy with school."

"And Jenny." Marcus wasn't doing a very good job of hiding his jealousy. "Don't forget about her."

"Well, you don't have to worry about her anymore." Mandy didn't bother trying to hide her bitterness. Or her guilt. "Pretty sure she never wants to see me again."

"You don't know that for sure."

"Well, she hasn't tried to reach out to me anywhere. And Bear said that her parents said they needed more time."

"They might need more time, but that doesn't mean Jenny does." Marcus sounded like a sage old wizard now. "Kids bounce back a lot faster. Maybe in a few months, she'll look back on the whole thing as a big adventure."

"*A few months?*" Mandy groaned. "We could be out of here by then."

"Well, you'll always have me."

"I know." Even through the phone, Mandy could sense Marcus blushing. "*Anyway,*" she said, throwing subtlety out the window, "let's see what other information we can get for Bear."

They worked for the next twenty minutes. Well, Marcus worked. Mandy just paced the house, grabbing snacks every couple of minutes and dragging them back to her room. She wasn't good at sitting still, but Marcus was the expert here.

About ten minutes into their hacking session, a couple text messages came through. Marcus took screenshots and sent them to Mandy, who forwarded them to Bear. If going to the house with the landline didn't work out, at least they had another lead. Though she wasn't doing much, Mandy felt better from being included at all. She only wanted to prove to Bear that she could help. That she could be an important part of the team.

Right now, she felt like Marcus was the MVP.

She tried not to be jealous. He'd offered to teach her what he knew multiple times in the last few months. It was just harder when she didn't always have a computer because she kept moving around when her dad was constantly looking over her shoulder. Bear wanted her to have a normal childhood, but she *wasn't* normal. And she was starting to think that was a good thing.

Jenny was great, and she did miss her, but Mandy wanted real adventure. As crazy as New York had been, she couldn't stop thinking about it. All the people they had helped. Sure, it was dangerous and scary. She did almost get kidnapped. But she'd never felt stronger than when she was able to get away on her own. Able to take care of herself.

Isn't that what Bear was always training her for? Why expose her to all of this, why teach her these skills, if he was never going to let her use them? She might only be fourteen, but she had already seen a lot more of the world—and the people in it—than most kids her age.

Fourteen wasn't that young. Soon, she'd be fifteen. Only three years from being a full-blown adult. What did parents always say? *They grow up so fast.* Mandy wondered if Bear would let her go off on her own at eighteen.

Then a more sobering thought landed with a thud.

Would Bear see her turn eighteen?

Sometimes Mandy thought Bear was invincible. He'd been shot and stabbed and nearly killed so many times, and he'd always gotten back up. Mandy knew luck and skill weren't always enough to survive. He'd had a *brain tumor*, and while he might've recovered from that, she sometimes noticed he wasn't the same. Especially after Sasha died.

Like all the other times Mandy's brain imagined Sasha, she tried to fight it. She didn't want to think about Sasha's last moments, about how they felt like a real family for that short amount of time. Bear had been happy, despite all the craziness in their lives. *She* had been happy. And the universe had snatched that away from them.

Didn't they deserve a break?

This is where the two sides of herself conflicted. Mandy wanted nothing more than freedom and adventure and the chance to prove to Bear that she remembered everything he'd taught her. She also liked the idea of a normal childhood, where her dad didn't get shot at and she could make friendships that would last a lifetime. It sounded safe. It sounded like a world where her dad would always be around.

"Aha!"

Mandy jumped and came crashing back to reality. She glared at Marcus for interrupting her very deep and important thoughts, but he was hardly paying attention. His fingers sped across his keyboard. "Find something?"

"That third number, finally. Whoever it belongs to, they didn't want to be found."

"I thought you said it was a local number?"

"It is, but *they* might not be. The signal was bouncing around all over the place so they're trying to cover their tracks. But with the *Marcusinator* on their heels—"

"For the tenth time," Mandy said, rolling her eyes. "That's not going to be your hacker name."

"Why not?"

"Because it's dumb."

"It's not dumb. It's *terrifying*. The Terminator is one of the greatest cinematic—"

Mandy stopped listening. She'd heard this speech before, but that's not why she'd tuned out. She could've sworn the front door had opened and swung closed again. Bear had locked it before he left—she'd triple-checked it like always—but there was no doubt in her mind that she'd heard the distinctive squeak of that hinge.

Mandy glanced at the clock on her phone. Bear had only been gone a half hour. Between the first place and the motel room, there was no way he'd be back here now. No way he wouldn't have called ahead in the first place.

Then who was downstairs? How had they gotten in?

The Murrays didn't have a key. It could've been the landlord, but Bear had said the guy lived on the mainland. Would he show up and let himself in without knocking? Maybe she hadn't heard the knock because of Marcus and his *Terminator* rant.

Mandy tuned back in to hear Marcus still monologuing.

"—and unlike a lot of people, I actually liked *Dark Fate*. Mackenzie Davis is an incredible action star, and I hope she—"

"Marcus, shut up."

He cut off and glared at her. "Well, that was rude. You could've just—"

She shushed him. "I think someone's inside my house."

He still. His eyes went wide. "What?" he whispered. "You need to get out of there."

"I'm putting you in my pocket. Mute yourself. I'm going to go investigate."

"Mandy, no."

"*Mute.*" She shoved the phone in her pants pocket. She didn't wait to see if he complied.

Prior to moving to Hatteras, Bear had bought Mandy a taser and taught her how to use it. It wasn't one of those cheap ones, either. The heavy-duty tool would incapacitate even the biggest guys. Bigger than Bear, anyway. After nearly getting kidnapped in New York, Bear thought she should have a weapon on her. Mandy had wanted a knife, but he'd said she wasn't ready.

The only problem was that she couldn't bring the taser to school. If she got caught with it, she'd be in serious trouble. As a result, the thing lived in the bottom drawer of her nightstand. Not very useful if she was coming home from school, but excellent if anyone was stupid enough to break into their house.

Mandy tried not to feel giddy at the idea of finally being able to use it. She should probably be scared right now, but she was too focused on what she wanted to tell Bear when he came home and found an intruder tied to the kitchen chair.

With that in mind, Mandy crept to her bedroom door, slowly twisted the handle, and cringed as it creaked open. She heard silence from downstairs, and for a moment, Mandy wondered if she'd imagined the whole thing.

The sound of shattering glass proved she'd been right all along.

35

BEAR PULLED INTO THE DRIVEWAY COCKEYED, NOT CARING THAT HE'D driven onto the grass. The house looked normal. Silent. Alarm bells still rang in his head, and he wouldn't shut them off until he held Mandy in his arms.

When he jumped out of his truck, his knees almost buckled beneath him. He was exhausted from the fights of the last couple days and the injuries Clint Michaels had inflicted. The knife wound still bled profusely, and Bear hadn't even attempted to wrap it or stem the blood. In his weakened state, he'd have to rely on adrenaline and sheer willpower if there was another attack.

Using the truck to steady himself, Bear stumbled up the front steps of the house. The front door was still closed. A good sign. He tested the handle. Locked. Either Doyle hadn't made it here yet, or he'd been smart enough to close the door behind him to put Bear at ease. Make him vulnerable. Bear knew too well not to let his guard down just yet.

He fished his keys out of his pocket, cursing when they slipped through his fingers and landed with a thud on the front porch. When he stooped to pick them up, his head swam, and he was forced to lean against the side of the house before he could regain all his senses. With a deep breath, he fit the key into the lock and twisted, swinging the door open ahead of him.

Bear waited for a count of three before stepping inside, brandishing the same knife that had inflicted the damage to his body. He expected Doyle to emerge from the kitchen, a gun held to Mandy's head, or for her to be screaming for help upstairs.

He heard nothing.

Bear clicked the door closed behind him but didn't lock it, in case they needed to make a quick getaway. Then he took one step forward. No one was in the kitchen, and Bear couldn't hear anything from upstairs. Not a single voice or footfall. But then—

The squeak of a hinge.

Bear whipped toward the sound. Too fast. He stumbled again, his head swimming and his whole body off balance. He threw an arm out to steady himself, knocking over a lamp in the process. The glass exploded across the floor in shards.

Footsteps on the stairs had him looking up, holding out the knife, not quite ready for whatever Doyle had in store for him, but willing to do anything to keep Mandy safe.

The figure on the stairs stopped halfway down, and it took Bear a second too long to realize it was Mandy, holding her taser out like she was ready to take on an army. When they saw each other, they both relaxed. A sigh escaped Bear's mouth, and he almost slumped to the ground in relief.

"What the hell happened to you?" Mandy continued down the rest of the stairs.

"Made some new friends," Bear said. His brain was catching up now. "What are you doing?"

"Thought you were an intruder."

"I know that." Bear straightened, some fire back in his body. "And you ran down the stairs to attack them? Instead of *running away like we discussed?*"

"Like you discussed," Mandy said, but at least she had the wherewithal to look guilty. When she spotted Bear's arm, she rushed over to him. "Seriously, what happened? Are you okay?"

She started patting his arms and chest. "We need to close this wound."

Bear waved her off. "I'll be fine. Doyle's on the way here. We need to get out."

"Not with you bleeding like this."

"We can do it somewhere else. Grab the kit. We need to go."

No sooner had the words left Bear's mouth than they heard a knock at the door. They both froze. Bear relaxed first. If it was Doyle, he sure as hell wasn't going to politely let them know he'd arrived. He strode across the room and looked through the peephole, then pulled the door open. Rosie was on the other side.

"We need to talk." She walked past Bear and gave Mandy a weak smile. "Now."

"Now's not a good time," Bear said. He closed the door behind her, then walked into the kitchen for a couple of rags. "I'll find you later."

"I'm being forced to sell," Rosie said. Her voice had ratcheted up an octave. "They don't want my money anymore. They want the shop. If I don't sign the contract, they're going after my sister and her kids. This just got a lot more serious, Bear."

"It's been serious," Bear said, grabbing a handful of ice from the freezer and holding it to his head.

Rosie finally registered Bear's appearance. "What the hell happened to you?"

"I asked him the same thing." Mandy put her hands on her hips. "All he said was he made some new friends."

Bear glared at her. "Go get the kit." He turned to Rosie as Mandy stomped back upstairs. "Doyle's not too happy with me at the moment. Go home."

"I'm not going anywhere," Rosie said. "We're safer in numbers."

Bear nodded his head. "Fine. Then get in the truck. We can't stay here. It's not safe. For anyone."

Rosie took his arm in her hands and lifted the rag from his wound. "You need to close this."

"Later. When we're safe."

Mandy returned with the kit and her go-bag less than sixty seconds later. She had her phone in one hand. Marcus was still on the line. "Bear, I think he found something."

"Later," Bear said, already tired of the word. He shuffled the other two through the door after making sure the coast was clear. Then he locked up behind him. Not that it would slow Doyle down. That was one of the problems with renting—he didn't have his own security system setup.

Mandy crawled into the backseat of the truck while Rosie climbed into the front. Bear swung himself into the driver's seat, tossing the bloody rags into the back with Mandy. "Buckle up."

Bear backed out into the street, narrowly missing a car parked opposite the Murray house. Mandy yelped when he straightened up and hit the gas, pinning her to the backseat. Rosie held onto the grab handle above the door to steady herself, but even she let out a little *oomph* as Bear turned a sharp corner without slowing down first.

"Bear, Marcus was telling me he found out who that last number belonged to. Some guy named—"

Bear wasn't listening. He only had eyes for the road. He didn't know where to go, but he knew he had to put as much distance between them and Doyle as possible. With the road to Avon still out, his options were limited.

"Your sister lives in Ocracoke?" Bear asked Rosie, cutting Mandy off.

"Yes, but—"

"Where?"

"We're not going there."

"We don't have a choice." Bear checked the rearview mirror. No one was following them. "What's the address?"

"I'm not telling you that." Rosie threw up the one hand that wasn't in a death grip around the grab handle. "Didn't you hear me? They're going to go after her. I have to stay as far away as possible."

"If we're there, we can protect her."

"She has *kids*, Bear. I'm not putting them in that situation."

Mandy piped up from the backseat again. "Bear, I really think you should listen to what Marcus found."

Bear had had enough. Without putting on his turn signal, he pulled off to the side of the road, not bothering to do a good enough job of it. His adrenaline levels were returning to normal, which meant there was a crash coming on. He wanted to be somewhere safe for that, but he couldn't concentrate with everyone talking and second-guessing and—

His phone rang.

Bear growled and fished it out of his pocket, fully intending to bite the head off of anyone else who dared to add one more thing to his plate. Panic squeezed his chest again when he saw the caller was Joseph Murray. If Doyle hadn't found him and Mandy at home, maybe he'd turned his sights to a new victim.

Bear picked up before it could ring again. "Joseph?"

Coughing came from the background. It sounded like Muriel. "Doyle attacked us." His voice was panicked and faint. It took all his effort to speak into the phone. He coughed three times before he could continue. "The house on fire. Muriel's hurt. I-I don't think I can carry her out. I called the fire department, but I don't think they'll get here in time. Bear"—he coughed—"help. Please."

Bear didn't hesitate for another second. He threw the truck into drive and made a wide U-turn, heading back the way they'd come.

"I'm on my way."

36

BEAR PARKED THE TRUCK A BLOCK AWAY IN CASE DOYLE PLANNED TO USE his attack on the Murrays as a distraction to get to Mandy. He also pulled out his pistol.

"You ever shoot before?" he asked Rosie.

She paled. "N-no."

Bear turned to Mandy, handing her the gun. "Keep the safety on until you see trouble. Remember to breathe. Focus your shot." She knew how to handle a weapon, but she'd never shot a person before. "If you pull that trigger—"

"—make sure I've got a good reason." Mandy's voice was solemn. "I know, Bear. I can do it."

"I'll be back." Bear looked between the two of them. "Lock the doors. Don't open up for anyone but me or the Murrays. Got it?"

"Yes," they both stammered.

Bear took one last look at Mandy, then slammed the door. He waited until he heard the locks click before he took off toward the house. His legs were tired, but he kept moving forward. His arm was bleeding less now, but the air itself made it throb in pain.

He sure as hell deserved a drink after this.

Had this been Doyle's plan all along, and he'd arrived before Bear had gotten to Mandy? Or had Doyle seen the trio leave and figured this was the next best solution? Not that it mattered. Not like it changed their circumstances.

Smoke filled the air now. Bear wondered if any of the neighbors were home. If any of them realized the fire could spread to their houses.

When he reached the front door, Bear tested the handle, lukewarm to the touch. The fire was either at the back of the house or upstairs. Either wasn't good for the structure or the Murrays, but it gave Bear a chance to get inside.

"Joseph?" Bear called out as soon as he stepped into the living room. "Joseph? Where are you?"

He heard a faint voice from upstairs. Bear ran to the stairs. Black smoke billowed across the second-floor ceiling, its acrid scent invading Bear's nose and mouth. His eyes watered as he tried to cough the soot out of his lungs, desperate for oxygen.

He should've grabbed a towel to put over his nose. No time now. He pulled his shirt over his nose and under his eyes, only a temporary solution. As soon as he needed both hands, he'd be screwed.

More yelling drove Bear farther up the stairs. He followed the noises until he came to a room at the end of the hall. Doyle had stuck a chair up under the handle to keep the Murrays locked in. Someone like Mandy or Bear might've been able to jump out of the window, but there was no way Joseph or Muriel could make the leap. Doyle meant to kill them.

Bear tossed the chair to the side and swung the door open. The dark smoke had already infiltrated the room. Now it rumbled into the hallway and down the stairs, happy to dig its dark claws into a new space.

Muriel lay on the floor on the far side of the room, crying and covering her face with a hand towel. Joseph knelt on the floor in front of her, a cane in one hand and another towel in the other. When he spotted Bear, his eyes widened with relief.

"Bear," he said, lowering the cloth just enough so Bear could hear him. "Thank God."

Bear rushed over to Muriel but hesitated to lift her. "Everyone okay?"

"He pushed me from behind," Muriel said. "I hit my head, but I was only out for a second. Nothing's broken."

"You sure?" Bear asked. He could make things worse by moving her. Not that he had a choice at this point.

"I'm sure." She looked up at him, more tears flowing down her cheeks. "I just want to get out of here."

The three heard a popping sound and a large crack. The room shook. Their time was running out. "Joseph, can you stand? Walk on your own?"

"Not sure. He pushed me too. Felt something in my hip pop. Hurts like a sonofabitch. Think I'll be okay, but I'm not gonna be fast." Joseph looked at his wife, then back to Bear. "Save her first. I can hold out."

Muriel gasped. "Joe, no—"

They didn't have time to argue. "Here's the plan," Bear said. "I'm carrying Muriel out of here. Shutting the door behind me. As soon as she's clear, I'm coming back for you. Seems like this room's opposite the fire, so you should be alright. Just hang tight, okay?"

"I don't know where Doyle is." Joseph shifted to a more comfortable position. "He dragged us up here, locked us inside. Then set the fire. He could still be around."

"If he's stupid enough to show his face again, I'll deal with him," Bear growled. He was ready to put an end to this.

Joseph nodded, and Bear eased Muriel to her feet. The smoke was thicker now, the popping and cracking louder. Bear made it to the hallway and swung the bedroom door shut behind him. When he turned back to the staircase, it was like a whole different world.

He could see the fire make its way through the beams along the wall and ceiling of the second floor. The smoke was so thick now, he could barely keep his eyes open. As one arm wrapped around Muriel and the other felt along the wall for guidance, he couldn't keep his shirt up over his nose.

Once they reached the edge of the stairs, they had another problem. Smoke billowed up from the ground floor now. Doyle had set a second blaze or the pop and crack they'd heard earlier was the floor falling through on one side of the house, allowing the fire to spread downstairs.

"We're gonna have to do this next part quick," Bear told Muriel between coughs. "Hold tight, okay?"

Bear felt the older woman nod next to him. He shifted his arms from her shoulders to her waist, then scooped her legs up and carried her down the stairs. They felt solid enough under his feet, but that could change in a heartbeat. Housefires had minds of their own. It only took mere minutes take a turn for the worst.

Muriel clung to Bear's neck. Though she was light, the lack of oxygen to Bear's lungs made it hard to ignore the exhaustion pulling at his limbs. Every time a cough wracked his chest, he felt like he lost some of his grip.

Bear stumbled at the bottom of the stairs but managed to keep his feet. He could feel heat behind him now. The fire had jumped from the rug to the curtains and some of the furniture. It'd be a full-blown inferno soon.

Bursting through the front door relieved his whole body. The smoke was still in his lungs and nose and mouth, but he could taste the outside air's saltiness. The ocean breeze was like a cool salve on his skin, and it cleared some of the tears from his eyes.

He set Muriel on the ground in the front yard, far enough away that she'd be safe. He turned to leave but Muriel called out to him, holding up the towel she'd had pressed to her face.

He took the towel and wrapped it around his head, charging back into the house. A couple neighbors rushed over to Muriel. He heard sirens in the distance, screaming closer with every passing second.

In the moment since Bear had left the house, the entire environment had changed once again. Fire licked the ceiling on the first floor and had claimed all the furniture. The flames grew taller as they consumed everything in sight.

Bear didn't waste time. He bounded up the stairs through thick smoke, working from memory as he made his way back to the bedroom.

Bear could feel the heat from the floorboards through the soles of his shoes. He didn't have much longer.

Joseph was on his feet when Bear burst into the room, leaning on his cane, and favoring his left leg. He'd tied his own towel around his face, but Bear could see the questioning look in his eyes.

"She's safe," he said. "Your turn."

Joseph didn't argue as Bear led him toward the door. He was larger than Muriel and Bear was twice as tired as he was moments ago. He wouldn't be able to carry the man down the stairs. Joseph knew the house better than Bear, so he took the lead while Bear made sure they both stayed on their feet.

About halfway down the stairs, everything changed. One minute, Bear stood upright. The next, his foot fell through the wood and he pitched forward. He lost his grip on Joseph, and the man went tumbling down the rest of the stairs, landing hard on the floor below. Bear could feel flames licking at his leg, melting his sneakers.

With a grunt of pain, Bear pulled his foot free and launched himself down the rest of the stairs, landing on his ankle and just barely keeping it from rolling. Joseph was already sitting up trying to use his cane as leverage. If anything was broken, he wasn't reacting to it. Maybe that was just the adrenaline.

The fire burned brighter, and Bear lifted Joseph back to his feet. Any pain they endured now would be worth it if they could just make it to the doorway.

As soon as they stepped over the threshold, a figure appeared in front of them. At first, Bear thought it was a concerned neighbor trying to help. Then the man shoved Joseph to the ground and shoved Bear back into the house. Doyle seethed with rage.

"I knew I should've killed you myself," Doyle spat, charging at him.

Bear tried to stay on his feet, but his energy was sapped. The smoke and heat were getting to his head. He landed on the floor with a grunt. Doyle wrapped his hands around Bear's throat and squeezed.

The man had been hiding out, away from the fire. Despite the smoke still swirling around them, Doyle's lungs were clear enough to let him breathe. The oxygen translated into enough energy to pin Bear to the ground and choke the life from him.

In that moment, Bear thought of Mandy. He hoped she had listened to him and stayed in the truck, but he wouldn't mind if she popped up with that pistol and used it to get Doyle off him. He never wanted Mandy to take a life if she could help it—especially at such a young age —but as Bear's vision began to fade, he couldn't stop himself from praying that she'd come to his rescue.

It wasn't Mandy who answered his prayer. It was Joseph, who swung his cane as hard as he could at Doyle's head. The other man toppled to the ground, and Bear used his remaining strength to haul himself to his feet just in time to watch part of the ceiling come down.

Bear ducked and ran toward the door, pulling Joseph with him. As soon as they cleared the doorway, two neighbors pulled the old man from the porch and steered him away from the house. Bear turned back around, knowing he couldn't let Doyle burn. Whether it was his morals or the fact that he still had questions, Bear didn't know. It didn't matter.

Bear stepped back inside the house, spotting Doyle underneath a burning pile of debris. The other man was trying to shove a beam from his leg, but it wouldn't give. He looked around in panic as the ceiling gave a final crack. Their eyes met for a split second before Doyle disappeared beneath the rubble.

37

BEAR STAYED LONG ENOUGH TO MAKE SURE THE MURRAYS WERE OKAY before slipping away from the crowd. He couldn't bring himself to feel too bad for how Doyle went out. The man had threatened Mandy. He'd tried to kill Joseph and Muriel. He would've killed Bear.

Everyone was too busy watching the spectacle to notice Bear leaving. The fire department had arrived and were dousing the flames. The house was gone. All the Murrays' possessions were reduced to rubble. They would still have their memories, but it would be a while until they were grateful for that.

When Bear rounded the corner and saw Mandy and Rosie in the truck, he finally allowed himself to relax. He wasn't sure if Doyle would've sent his men after them while Bear was distracted by the fire. They'd gotten lucky.

When Bear climbed inside, the women stared wide-eyed at his disheveled state. He was covered in dirt and soot, and he smelled worse than a campfire. He was still cut up from his earlier run-in with Doyle and the guys at the motel, and now he had a sore ankle and a burnt pant leg. The little energy he had left was disappearing fast.

"Bear, you need to get cleaned up," Mandy said.

He didn't bother arguing. "We need somewhere safe."

"I know where to go," Rosie said.

Bear put the truck into drive and awaited her instructions. It wasn't until they were pulling into the deli parking lot that he realized where she was taking them. And what it meant for her to bring him here. If he wasn't so dead tired, he might've been grateful.

"We're getting food?" Mandy peered through the windshield at the back of the sandwich shop.

"Only if you ask nicely," Rosie teased.

Bear stumbled out of the truck, his ankle twinging in protest. Mandy was there in seconds, scooping one of his arms over her shoulders. She wasn't carrying much of his weight, but he took comfort in her presence.

Rosie knocked twice on the back door. A moment later, it opened. A short Italian man with a bad combover and an impressive mustache stood on the other side. His eyes narrowed at the two strangers, and he looked to Rosie for answers.

"We need a place to hide. He can help us."

The man looked at Bear for a moment, taking in his disheveled appearance. Something in Bear's appearance made him look trustworthy. The other man nodded once and stepped to the side, letting the trio in. He locked the door behind him.

"Sit there," he said, pointing to barstool in the corner. "Try not to bleed on anything."

Bear settled himself on the stool as the owner made his way out front. The seat was far from comfortable, but it beat standing, and he was able to lean his head against the wall. Although there was little chance he wouldn't bleed on anything, they at least appeared to be in some sort of back room and not the kitchen area. Like a parlor for card games or clandestine meetings.

"That's Sal," Rosie said. "He's grumpy, but he's got a good heart. Kind of like you."

"I'm not grumpy," Bear grumbled, but he didn't have it in him to be convincing.

"You're the grumpiest person I've ever met." Mandy swung her backpack off her shoulders, retrieving their med kit. "And I've met some pretty grumpy people."

Bear closed his eyes, trying to focus on anything but the pain he felt throughout his body. Cuts and scrapes and burns and sore muscles—all of it congealed into one large ache that sent electric currents through his body. He could sleep for days, but there was still too much to do.

Mandy patched up Bear with practiced perfection. She'd been doing it a long time, and this was hardly the worst scrape Bear had ever been in. With some water and a clean cloth, she wiped most of the dirt from Bear's limbs, then applied butterfly stitches to the worst cuts. They had ointment for the burns, which didn't look bad enough to be concerned about.

All in all, it took her about twenty minutes to get him back in working condition. By that time, Rosie had called in reinforcements. Sal had closed up shop and made sandwiches for the three of them. Bear was wolfing his down when the rest of the resistance group arrived. Fewer people had shown up for this emergency meeting than when Bear barged in on them, but it was enough. Every little bit helped.

Rosie introduced them one at a time. Kate and Marie Watson were sisters in their fifties who had lived here their whole lives. Craig Livingston, a middle-aged construction worker, had been on the island for the last fifteen years. Joey Nizari was a twenty-something college dropout who had found wild success writing romance novels and decided to move to Buxton to enjoy the ocean. Lola Ferragni was Sal's niece, who had moved back to Hatteras after her divorce. Then there was Zeke, who came in last, holding the two items Bear had requested: a new set of clothes and a full bottle of whiskey.

"Not top shelf or anything," Zeke said, "but it'll take the edge off."

"I'd drink paint thinner right now," Bear said, taking the gifts. "Thanks for this."

Zeke waited until Bear returned from changing in the tiny bathroom before addressing the group. "I talked to the Murrays, too. They're on a boat heading up to the hospital in Rodanthe. It's just a precaution.

They've inhaled some smoke, and they're both pretty sore, but the paramedic said they should both be fine." He turned to Bear. "You're the reason why they're alive. Thank you. They're good people. They didn't deserve that."

"No one does," Kate said, wiping a tear away. Her sister squeezed her shoulder.

"Except maybe the people who set it on fire," Joey said. She was eyeing Bear's bottle of whiskey, so he held it out to her. She grabbed a glass, pouring herself a couple fingers. "Thanks."

"Andrew Doyle set the fire." Bear took the bottle back, not bothering with a glass himself. "He's dead."

Silence filled the room. Joey was the first one to speak. "Good riddance."

"You shouldn't say that," Kate said.

Joey shrugged. "But I did. He's been a pain in our ass for months. I'm not sad about it. Are you?"

Kate looked away.

"On that note," Bear said, shifting on the stool. "How are you guys involved in all this?"

"We've all lived here our whole lives or have known someone who has," Zeke said. "We've seen this place change. Noticed when someone started buying up property, and not selling it back. Some of us have businesses, like Rosie and Marie. And Sal, obviously. Guys started coming around and harassing us. When we realized some of us felt the same way, we formed this group."

"The Citizen's Brigade?" Bear asked.

Zeke rolled his eyes. "You've been talking to Jed."

"He got his privileges taken away," Joey said. "One too many drunken outbursts."

"You've had a few of those too," Craig said. Joey saluted him with her glass.

"We don't really have a name," Zeke said. "Didn't seem important at the time."

"What is important," Joey said, "is figuring out our next step." She slammed back the rest of her whiskey.

Mandy cleared her throat after a beat of silence. "I might have an idea." Bear quirked an eyebrow in her direction, and she pulled her phone from her pocket. Marcus was still on the line. "He figured out who that third number belongs to."

"Anyone we know?" Bear asked.

"Actually, yes" Marcus said from Mandy's phone. "Sending you the info now. It wasn't easy to track him down. Seems like he has multiple aliases. But I'm pretty sure this is his real name."

Bear pulled out his own phone and waited for the text to come through. "Rowan Salazar," Bear said. "I'm guessing he's not Terry Matthews' twin brother."

"They're one and the same," Marcus said.

Joey leaned over the table to look at Mandy's cell phone. Then she looked back up at Bear. "I'm sorry, do you have a ten-year-old on your payroll?"

"He doesn't get paid," Bear said.

"And I'm fourteen," Marcus added.

Joey held up her hands and backed away.

Rosie leaned over to look at Bear's cell. "You know him?"

"He owns a house on the canal. Paid him a visit earlier today. He said Doyle's been harassing him to sell, but he's refused. Seemed like a normal guy." Bear looked down at Rowan's picture. "But I think he knows more than he's letting on."

"Then let's find out what he knows," Mandy said.

"You're not going," Bear said. "Stay here, keep working with Marcus. See if you can dig up anything on Rowan. Make sure you look through his other aliases too."

"What are you going to do?" Rosie asked.

"Probably something stupid," Bear said, getting to his feet. The food had given him some energy, and the whiskey had loosened him up and dulled the pain. "I'll figure something out."

"I'll go with you." Zeke stepped forward. "Better to not be stupid alone."

Bear looked the man up and down. He didn't know Zeke well, but he seemed like the unofficial leader of the group. Maybe he'd be able to

offer Bear some more insight into what was going on around the island.
"How are you in a fight?" Bear asked.

"I can hold my own."

"Good enough for me."

38

ZEKE HAD OFFERED TO DRIVE, BUT BEAR DECIDED HE SHOULD concentrate on the road instead of how much the cut on his arm still burned from the alcohol Mandy had cleaned it with. It might've been smarter to take Zeke's small Kia Rio since he had a feeling his opponents were starting to recognize his truck, but there was something comforting in hopping behind the wheel of an F150 when it felt like the world was against you.

"Where are we heading first?" Zeke asked, once they were on the road.

"To check up on a friend," Bear said.

Bear could count on one hand the number of people on Hatteras that he cared about, and that last finger belonged to the reporter, Ben Carroll. They hadn't known each other long but they'd both been friends with Rosie's brother—and he'd been digging into this drug trafficking problem on the island for some time now—it seemed prudent to make sure no one had paid him a visit.

"Building's not on fire," Bear said as he pulled into the parking lot. "That's a good sign."

Zeke remained silent as the pair exited the truck and walked up to the Island Free Press' front door. Just like last time, Ben appeared to be the only one working. Unlike last time, the intrepid journalist was all too happy to see Bear at the door.

When he unlocked it for Bear and spotted Zeke, his face fell. The air around them grew thick with tension. It was only when Bear cleared his throat that the two realized he was still standing there.

"I take it I don't need to introduce you two?" Bear asked.

"No," Ben said. "We've known each other a long time."

Bear didn't miss the heavy meaning in his voice. "Can we come in?"

Ben hesitated, looking Zeke up and down again, before he stepped back and allowed them to enter. Bear followed Ben back to his desk, Zeke trailing behind him. Neither looked like they wanted to be the first one to break the silence, but the tension was getting on Bear's nerves. They had shit to do.

"Let's cut to the chase. What is this?" Bear pointed between the two of them."

Ben raised an eyebrow in Zeke's direction, but the other man looked away. Ben let out a bitter laugh. "Figures. Did Zeke ever tell you he was friends with Reed, too?"

Bear looked at the man standing next to him. "No, he did not."

"Didn't know I had to divulge the identity of every person I've ever passed on the street."

"Except Reed wasn't a passing acquaintance." Ben crossed his arms over his chest and turned back to Bear. "When Reed came back to Buxton, he and Zeke were buddies right away."

"You say that like we hadn't gone to high school together," Zeke cut in.

"But you weren't friends back then. Not as close as we were." He was still talking to Bear. "We all knew Reed had a drug problem. And a drinking problem. Zeke was usually the one egging him on, getting him to go out to bars."

"Look, I'm not a saint, okay?" Zeke was looking anywhere but at the two of them. "I had my own issues. I'm not proud of how I acted. But I turned things around in the end."

"That makes one of you."

Zeke looked up. "What's that supposed to mean?"

"Reed was drowning, and he was reaching out for help. Instead of throwing him a life preserver, you called the cops on him."

Zeke's face turned to stone. "Are you saying I'm the reason he's dead?"

Ben shrugged. "If the shoe fits."

Bear stepped forward before Zeke could lunge at Ben. "Had I known you guys had bad blood, I would've left him out in the truck." Bear waited until the two men looked away from each other. He turned back to Ben. "I just came to check in on you. Things are getting hot."

"How hot?"

"Doyle-set-the-Murrays'-house-on-fire hot." Bear held up his hand before Ben could ask the obvious question. "They're both fine. On the way to the hospital. Doyle got trapped in the house. He's dead."

"I suppose I should feel bad about that," Ben said.

"Don't waste too much energy on it." Bear gestured to the desk. "I came to see if you had anything for me. And to warn you to keep your eyes peeled."

"You think someone will come after me?"

Bear shrugged. "You've been digging into this for a while now, right? And we've met twice before. These guys seem to know who I'm friendly with in this town, so yeah. Just be smart about it."

"Point taken." Ben walked back around his desk and sat down in his chair. "I got the pictures, and you're right. This sub transported drugs."

Zeke perked up. "A sub?" He turned to Bear. "You didn't mention anything about that."

"Wanted to make sure I was right before I brought it up." Bear gestured for Ben to go on. "Find anything to point us in the right direction?"

"If you're looking for the guy's name and address, no." Ben looked disappointed. "These things are homemade, so it's not like there's a manufacturing company. The signs and instructions were written in Spanish, but there's no way to tell what country it came from."

"Where is this thing now?" Zeke asked. "Maybe we could go check it out."

Bear shook his head. "It's at the bottom of the Sound."

"I've got a friend who dives in the Sound. He's pretty good at finding stuff."

"Give him a call. I'll send you the sub's last known location. Maybe we'll find something else inside." Bear pulled out his own cell phone. "You know a guy named Rowan Salazar?"

Ben shook his head. "Can't say that I do."

"What about Terry Matthews?"

Ben paused. "Hang on." He clicked around on his computer and typed in a few letters. "Actually, yeah. He owns a house right on the canal. Said he'd been getting harassed. When I told him I'd like to interview him about his experience, he shut me down. Didn't want anything to do with me after that." Ben looked up at Bear. "Why?"

"Rowan and Terry are the same guy. I'm thinking he knows more than he's letting on. We're about the pay him another visit. You know anything else that could be useful?"

"He bought that house a couple years ago. Had a whole lot of construction done on it. People notice, you know? Neighbors talk. No one could figure out what he was doing. Construction workers were there for about eighteen months, but it never seemed like they were doing much work. Doesn't take that long to knock a wall down."

"You ever do any digging into the construction company?"

"No, but now I'm thinking I should."

Bear turned toward the door. "Let me know if you find anything."

39

As they headed over to the house on the canal, Bear noticed Zeke was upset. He didn't have to be a psychic to read the room. He cut a glance over at the other man, then returned his gaze to the road. "What's on your mind?"

Zeke sighed. "Don't understand why you didn't tell us about the sub."

"Didn't know who to trust."

"You didn't even tell Rosie?"

"Rosie was there." Bear cut another glance at the man. "Kind of surprised she didn't tell you."

Zeke stilled, then blew out a breath and relaxed. "She and I are figuring out how to become friends again. It hasn't been easy, and she doesn't always open up to me."

"Because of Reed?"

"Yeah."

Bear wasn't sure how much he should push. He couldn't get a good read on Zeke yet. The man commanded respect when he walked into a room, but he wasn't sure how Zeke had earned that. Bear didn't think it had anything to do with fear. He presented himself as someone who could get the job done. Sometimes that was enough.

In the end, Bear didn't have to press him for more information. Zeke divulged it himself.

"I don't want you to get the wrong idea about me." Zeke adjusted in his seat and looked out the passenger window. "About what happened with Reed."

"You're talking about what Ben said?"

Zeke nodded. "I understand why he's mad at me. Maybe I deserve it. Still hurts when I hear it."

"What happened?"

"He was right about Reed and I not being friends in high school. We ran in different circles. I was the jock, and he was the loner. Everyone liked him, but he wasn't loyal to one group, you know? And he used to do stupid shit for attention."

"Yeah, that sounds like him." Bear caught Zeke with a questioning look on his face. "We used to be friends when we were kids. Young kids. Hadn't seen him in a couple decades." He paused. "I was sad to hear he'd died. He deserved better than that."

"Most people do." Zeke studied Bear for a moment longer before looking away. "He left, and I continued the way I was. Got married. Had a couple kids. But that life was stifling. Don't get me wrong, I love my family," he said, rushing forward. "I'm grateful to them, but I was just tired of fitting into the box everyone expected me to stand in."

"That where the drugs came in?"

Zeke nodded. "Alcohol made life a lot more interesting. Made me more interesting. Not everyone got that. But Reed did."

"Did you know he was into the harder stuff?"

Zeke hesitated. Shifted in his seat again. Looked back out the window. "Yeah. Did it with him a couple times, but I didn't like the person it turned me into. I didn't realize how bad Reed was until the end. And if I could go back—" He broke off and cleared his throat before continuing. "If I could go back, I'd do it differently, you know?"

Bear turned a corner and waited until he straightened the truck back out before asking what had been on his mind for the last fifteen minutes. They were close to the house now, and he wanted answers. "What happened that night?"

Zeke bowed his head to look at his hands clasped together in his lap.

"Reed was looking to get help. To get clean. He'd also been depressed. He and his sisters weren't talking much. He'd gotten into some trouble with his supplier. I was afraid he was going to do something stupid."

"Like kill himself?"

Zeke nodded. "I called the cops to do a wellness check, but he freaked out. Apparently pulled a gun on them. They shot him in self-defense." He shook his head. "If I'd known Rosie had been there the whole time, I wouldn't have called them. I was just trying to help."

Bear pulled the truck over, just down the road from the canal house. "Now you guys are trying to figure out who his supplier was and get them to stop coming to Hatteras."

"It feels like the least I could do for Reed."

"Let's get it done," Bear said.

He didn't have a plan other than trying to catch Rowan off guard. There was no point in trying to sneak into the house. If the cops got involved, Bear would be on the wrong side of the situation. Plus, Rowan would know that they knew something was up.

No, it was best to just knock on the front door, ask the man some questions, and then use his considerable bulk to get Rowan to answer them. Though Rowan wasn't small by any measure, he wouldn't have a chance against the two men.

If he was alone, that is.

When Bear and Zeke climbed the stairs to the porch, they saw the front door was cracked open. They exchanged a look, then Bear took the lead, drawing out his pistol and keeping it pointed down. If Zeke was bothered by the fact that Bear had a gun, he didn't say anything.

Bear pushed the door open and stepped inside. The house was quiet and smelled like the ocean. That was probably normal for a house on the canal, but it struck him as odd that there were no other scents— Rowan's lunch, dirty shoes, dusty carpets. None of it. The house smelled empty and unused.

The living room looked as Bear remembered it, with matching blue and brown furniture. He'd been right the first time—it was new and expensive. And unused. A detail he had missed previously. The tags were still on it, and it looked just as stiff as it would've on day one.

It was just for show.

Bear's suspicions were confirmed when he walked into the kitchen. There was nothing in there. No appliances, no towels, not even a garbage can. The cupboards were empty. Rowan had never once used it to cook his lunch.

"This is strange," Zeke said.

"You're telling me." Bear walked through the rest of the empty house. "Either Rowan cleaned out everything but the living room furniture, or he never lived here to begin with."

"Any idea what he was doing here then?"

"Could've just been a storage unit for the drugs," Bear said, "but why go to the trouble of furnishing one room? Why convince all your neighbors that you live here?"

They returned to the living room. Zeke bent down to inspect the furniture more closely. "So that when he opened the front door, the house looked like it was lived in." Bear grunted in approval, his mind still spinning as Zeke pushed the couch to the side and peeled up the area rug underneath. "Or to better hide something."

Bear walked over to what looked like a trap door in the middle of the floor. It was just big enough for a man his size to fit through, but he couldn't figure out where it could possibly go. The house was built on a canal. The room couldn't be a basement of any sort. It was most likely a secret tunnel out of the house.

"Stay behind me." Bear held onto his gun with one hand and used the other to flip the door open. A putrid scent hit them both in the face, and Bear had to take a few seconds to adjust to the odor of rotting fish. Then he descended the stairs, Zeke on his heels.

The stairs weren't long. Before Bear knew it, he was standing on wet dirt underneath the house. The entire area was open, and on three sides, the siding from the house extended all the way to the ground. Track marks in the mud led to the fourth side, facing the canal, and that's when Bear put it all together.

"The subs would come up the canal with the drugs. The water's just deep enough that they could stay under the surface without anyone noticing. Then they'd navigate to that opening right there." He walked closer, feeling his feet sinking deeper into the sticky mud. "That's where they'd unload everything and bring it up to the house. This wasn't just for storage." He turned back to Zeke. "This is their offloading zone."

"God, what is that smell?" Zeke tried to hold his breath. "Rotten fish?"

Bear had thought so too, but it was too strong, too twisted to be fish. He walked closer to the opening. He could see the water now, lapping up to the edge of the house. He could also see the dead body floating face down, just off to the side. Bear had no idea how long it had been there, but it was bloated and distorted.

Bear heard the other man gasp when he spotted it. "Do you think that's Rowan?" Zeke answered.

"Don't think so. This guy looks darker and shorter." Still, he couldn't help himself. He had to check. Maybe all their problems had been solved for them.

When Bear knelt next to the body, he knew it wasn't Rowan. It was hard to tell much about him at all. Good for Rowan. Bad for them. And bad for this guy, whoever he was. There was rope tied to his arms and legs. "They let him drown here."

"Think Rowan did that?"

"Or one of his men," Bear mused. Any further thoughts were interrupted by his cell phone going off. He fished it out of his pocket. It was Mandy. "Hey, what's up?"

"Are you alone?" she asked.

"No, I've got Zeke here. What's up?"

"Bear, you gotta get out of there."

He stilled. "Is everything okay?"

"No." Mandy took a shuddering breath. "Marcus was digging into the resistance members, just to make sure they were who they said they were. Zeke's didn't match up."

As soon as Bear fully comprehended her words, he felt the barrel of a gun pressed to the back of his head.

Zeke's voice turned snide and cruel. "I'd hang up the phone if I were you."

40

"I said, hang up the phone."

"Okay, okay." Bear made a show of hanging up on Mandy. He knew she would be out of her mind with worry, but it was better to do what Zeke wanted. "It's done."

"Throw your phone into the water." When Bear hesitated, Zeke pressed the gun harder to the back of Bear's head. "Do it."

Bear threw the phone underhand, lobbing it so it would land in the shallows. It'd probably be enough to keep the device alive, and Zeke knew it. He growled from behind Bear.

"That was a stupid thing to do."

"Wasn't intention, man," Bear lied. "You've got a gun to my head. I'm nervous. Fingers slipped."

"Bullshit."

Bear shrugged. "I could go grab it if you want me to try again."

"Hook a finger through the trigger of your gun. Pass it back to me."

Bear did as he was told. Zeke was smarter than he looked. Bear would be smart not to agitate him, but it wasn't in his nature. "What next? Should I drop my pants too?"

"Don't fuck with me. I'm not in the mood."

"Okay." Bear kept his hands up in surrender. "Mind if I turn around?" Bear didn't wait for Zeke's answer. He turned slowly, in case Zeke got any ideas to end this quickly. "If I'm gonna go out like this, I at least want to look you."

Zeke sneered. "How honorable." He'd moved back a couple steps. Out of Bear's immediate reach, but not far enough. "Gotta admit, this is satisfying. Never really liked you, but Rosie did. She vouched for you every chance she got. I knew we'd have to bring you in at some point. You'd been sniffing around long enough as it was. But this worked out perfectly in the end."

Bear's eyes searched the ground for his gun and found it a couple feet away. Too far to be of any use to him. "So, you've been a traitor this whole time."

"More like a double agent." Bear finally caught the coldness in Zeke's eyes. The man was a good actor. "We had to make sure their little rebellion didn't mess with any of our plans."

"You mean Rowan's plans?" Bear asked. "I assume he called the shots."

"I know what you're doing, trying to goad me like that. It's not going to work. I'm happy with my lot in life. Got all the money I'll ever need, and if the empire falls, Rowan's going with it. Not me."

"So, this is all about money?"

Zeke shrugged. "And drugs. I like those, too."

"You're an addict. Didn't stop when Reed died."

"Not an addict. Addicts don't have any self-control. Like Reed." Zeke rolled his eyes. "He never could keep his shit together. I partake to unwind. But I never let it get out of control."

"Okay, so you're not an addict." Bear assessed Zeke while he talked. The gun didn't shake, but it was also pointed at Bear's chest, not his head. Zeke could hit him in the shoulder and not kill him, whereas any bullet to the face would put an end to Bear instantly. "Are you a killer?"

Zeke appeared proud of himself. He used his chin to point at the guy behind Bear. "Killed him, didn't I?"

Bear couldn't stop the way his eyebrows shot up. "Killed him? Or let him die? There's a difference."

Zeke took an aggressive step forward. The gun rose to point at Bear between the eyes. "The little bitch almost got us caught. Killed his buddy and threw him overboard. His body washed up. People started asking questions. Rowan gave me a job, and I did what I had to do."

"The Colombian who washed up on shore," Bear said. "They were the drug runners. Only this guy didn't deliver the drugs where he was meant to. The sub was sinking and he had to land up the beach."

"Like I said, he almost got us caught. He needed to pay the price."

"And like I said," Bear repeated, "there's a difference between killing someone and letting him die. I saw the ropes. You tied him down and let him drown, didn't you?"

"A horrible way to die."

"And pretty different from putting a bullet between someone's eyes." Bear's arms were starting to get tired. He'd have to make his move soon, but the mud was deep here, and his shoes were pretty stuck. "Have you ever done that?"

"There's a first time for everything."

Bear started to slip one of his feet free. "You've never shot someone," Bear said, ticking everything off on his fingers. "You drowned this guy. You called the cops on Reed. I guess that was intentional?"

"Reed was an idiot. He could've set himself up with the perfect life. Then he grew a conscience. He wanted to get *clean*." Zeke jabbed the gun forward to emphasize the word. "He wanted to expose the whole operation. We couldn't let that happen."

"You've been in this for a while then," Bear said, starting to slip his other foot free. "A couple years. No wonder you don't want it to go under."

"We own this island."

"You mean Rowan does."

Zeke ground his teeth together. "You're walking a thin line, man. I *will* end you."

"Why haven't you?" Bear asked. Then it came to him. "You're still trying to figure out how to play this with the group? You don't want them to get suspicious."

"Rosie won't like it if you wind up dead, and she's already mad at me for blowing up the road."

Bear chuckled. "So, she did know about that. She sent me after Ethan Gray. Said he and his guys did it. I guess she wasn't all that wrong. Just didn't know you were working for the other team."

"And she never will." Zeke shook his head. "Screw it. I'll figure out what to do after you're dead."

Bear barely let Zeke finish his sentence before he used every ounce of his remaining energy to sprint forward and tackle him to the ground. He pushed Zeke's arm up and away just in time for the gun to go off and slip out of Zeke's hands, putting a hole through the floor of the house. The sound echoed around the open space. Both men flinched.

Even though Bear was bigger, Zeke managed to get his leg between the two of them and push. Between the extra momentum and the slippery mud, Bear fell backwards, landing on his back. Something hard poked him between the shoulder blades, and it took him a few seconds to realize it was his gun.

Zeke was recovering quickly, sitting up and searching for his own weapon. Both were covered in mud. Zeke had some in one eye, desperately trying to wipe it away with the back of his hand while he scrambled for the gun.

Bear rolled over and grabbed his pistol, raising it at the same time Zeke raised his. They were only feet apart now. There was no chance either of them missed. It would all come down to timing.

Bear didn't hesitate.

He put his finger on the trigger and pulled. A shot rang out. Time slowed down. Bear waited to see if he felt any pain. To see if everything would fade to black. He thought of Mandy, and where she would end up if he died. She knew what to do if something like that happened. He still hated the idea that she'd be with anyone but him.

Not that it mattered. Bear's bullet found its target, hitting Zeke between the eyes. Shock crossed his face for a moment before slackening. He slumped backwards into the mud, the gun falling from his hand.

Bear got to his feet, kicking the gun away from Zeke's body and checking his pulse. Zeke was dead. Bear dragged the body a few feet into the water and shoved as hard as he could. After the body sunk below the surface, Bear trekked through the mud and scooped up his shoes and phone. By some miracle, it still worked. He dialed Mandy's number. She picked up on the first ring.

"Bear?" He could hear the frantic tone of her voice. "Are you okay?"

"I'm fine."

"And Zeke?"

Bear looked down at the body. "Dead."

Mandy breathed a sigh of relief. "I was so scared when you hung up. But no one let me come after you. And Rosie didn't want to believe what I'd found."

"Tell them I'm on my way back. We've got some things to talk about."

41

BEAR WASHED UP THE BEST HE COULD IN THE DELI'S SINK. HE MANAGED TO get most of the mud off his skin and the bigger chunks out of his borrowed clothes, but he still looked a mess. The bathroom wasn't much better. He'd apologize to Sal for that later. Right now, if he couldn't get a proper shower, he at least wanted a proper drink. Another, that is.

When he returned to the back room, everyone else was still there. They all looked somber. Bear had given them the rundown of what had happened between him and Zeke. No one looked particularly sorry, though he did catch Kate wiping tears from her eyes.

Before anyone spoke, Bear grabbed the whiskey and pulled from the bottle. He sat it back down in front of Joey and grabbed a chair next to Mandy. She gave him a half grin in response. Bear knew how she felt—relieved he was okay, but not looking forward to what came next. He looked at Rosie, who was staring at him with apprehension. He didn't want to do this in front of the rest of the group, but it didn't look like he had any other choice. The time for secrets was over.

"Did you know?" Bear asked Rosie.

"Know what?"

"That Zeke was a mole."

"No, I didn't." Rosie's eyes were wide. Scared. "I swear I didn't. I had no idea he was going after you like that."

"You knew about the bomb. You knew he wanted to blow up the road."

There were gasps around the room. Joey leaned forward over her new glass of whiskey. "I must've misheard you. Can you say that again?"

Rosie looked down at her feet. "I knew Zeke planted the bomb." She flinched when Joey stood up out of her chair. "He told me it was the only way to cut the suppliers off. We needed to send them a message."

"My guess is it didn't slow them down at all," Bear said. "They were bringing product in through the canal."

Joey was staring daggers at Rosie. "You said it was Ethan Gray and his people. You both convinced us it was some sort of retaliation for the moves we'd been making. That it was a warning. That's why we've been laying low."

"That's what he told me to say." Rosie looked the other woman in the eyes, and Bear could see genuine fear and regret. "He said you guys wouldn't understand."

Joey sat back down and took a swig of whiskey. "Well, he had that part right at least."

"He did it for my brother." Rosie turned to Bear. "He wanted to punish those responsible for his death."

Bear wasn't sure he wanted to be the one to break the news to her, but Rosie deserved to know the truth. "Those guys might've put the drugs in your brother's hands, but Zeke was the one who called the cops on him."

"It was an accident." Rosie was sobbing now. "He didn't mean to get him killed."

"Reed was going to clean up his act. He was gonna go to the cops and try to bring the whole operation down. Zeke found out, and he couldn't let that happen. He was making too much money. He wasn't trying to get Reed killed, but he *was* trying to shut him up. Either way, he didn't regret calling the cops." Bear looked around the room. "He told me himself. He had no reason to lie, not when he thought I'd be dead."

"Good riddance," Marie spat, and Kate looked at her sister like she'd grown a second head. "What? I refuse to mourn a man who manipulated us at every turn. He'd sooner throw one of us under the bus. Better him than me or you or anyone else in this room."

"A man is still dead," Kate said, shaking her head. "It should never end like that."

"But it did." Marie looked at Bear. "What are you going to do about that?"

"I killed him in self-defense," Bear said. "Once the cops get the full picture, they'll see that."

"What about her?" Joey asked, cutting a look at Rosie. "We can't trust her anymore."

"She didn't do anything wrong," Kate said. "She was manipulated just like the rest of us."

"She lied to us."

Rosie sobbed now. Perhaps shock had set in. "I-I'm sorry. I didn't know. I-I never would've—" She broke off as another sob climbed its way up her throat. "If I had known what he'd done, what he'd *been* doing, I never would've gone along with it." She looked up at Bear. "You have to believe me."

"I'm not the one you need to convince."

Hurt flashed across Rosie's face before she turned to Sal. "Please."

Sal placed a hand on her shoulder. "I believe you, but it's going to take time for us to heal. Zeke pulled the wool over everyone's eyes. We have to figure out what this means for us. What's next."

"Yeah," Joey said, looking at Bear. "What's next?"

"Hell if I know," Bear said.

He wanted to pack up and leave right then and there. Doyle had been the face of this campaign—bullying everyone left and right. He was out of the picture now. As far as Bear was concerned, he'd done his job. Zeke had made a move, and Bear had reacted to keep himself alive. He was glad Zeke had been outed as the mole, but he didn't relish the idea of adding another body to the mental list he kept.

Bear looked down at Mandy, who wore an expression of relief mixed with concern. He'd taught her to finish what she started. What kind of example would he be setting if he let Rosie, Sal, Joey, and the others deal with the rest of this on their own? They weren't equipped for what was coming their way, but he was.

Before Bear could figure out his next steps, his phone rang. He looked down at the display. This was the last person he'd expected to hear from. "Ethan Gray," Bear said. Everyone else in the room sat up straighter. "To what do I owe the pleasure?"

"What the hell did you do?" Ethan asked. He sounded out of breath.

"You have to be a little more specific. In the last twenty minutes or the last twenty-four hours?"

"Cut the bullshit. Give me the cliff notes. Everyone is freaking out here. I'm just trying to protect my kids."

Bear sighed. He didn't like the guy, but he didn't want anything bad to happen to his family. "Doyle set a fire and almost killed the Murrays. Found out Zeke was working for you guys the whole time. Both of them tried to kill me. And considering you're talking to me and not either of them, you can deduce how that ended."

Ethan swore. "You kicked the hornet's nest. I hope you know what you're doing."

"Where's Rowan?"

Ethan was silent for a minute. "How do you know that name?"

"I won't tell you that," Bear said. Not least because he'd gotten it from a fourteen-year-old kid. "But I will tell you that if you give me his location, I'll end this. Your family will be safe."

Ethan hesitated for a single breath. "He's got a boat at Oden's Dock. Named the *Andromeda*. I'd bet money he's heading for the Pamlico River, trying to get the hell out of dodge. Like the rest of us."

"I hope you have a good lawyer, Gray." Bear meant that. "Your kids deserve to grow up with their father."

"In a different life, I think we'd be friends, Mr. Logan. It's almost a shame."

"Almost." Bear chuckled. "Hope I don't see you around."

"Me neither." There was a brief pause. "End this." Then the line went dead.

Bear shoved his phone back in his pocket. "Rowan is heading to

Oden's Dock. I've got to cut him off before he gets to the river. If he makes it back to land, we'll never catch him."

"My brother's got a boat at the docks," Craig said.

Bear's adrenaline kicked up. This was it. "Tell him we're gonna need to borrow it."

42

CRAIG KEPT A SPARE BOAT KEY ON HIM AT ALL TIMES. WHATEVER hesitation the man felt about not telling his brother what they were up to was washed away by the desire to get Rowan once and for all. Bear promised he'd keep the boat safe, but he'd do what it took to take this guy down.

Besides, he could buy Craig's brother a new boat. A better one.

Not that the one he owned was all that bad. It was a little smaller than the Picketts', but it was also newer and faster. It had been named the *Serendipity*. Despite it not being brand new, there wasn't a scratch or stain on it. He hoped that wouldn't change today.

Oden's Dock was south of Buxton, about fifteen minutes away. Bear made it in ten. Rowan had still beaten him to the docks by about a minute. He was already pulling out into open water by the time Bear jumped onto the *Serendipity* and started it up. Rowan's boat, the *Andromeda*, was bigger and more cumbersome than the *Serendipity*. On straight stretches, Rowan could outpace Bear, but there were too many obstacles in the Pamlico Sound. Bear could take sharper turns. He just had to get Rowan to make a single mistake. That's when he'd strike.

Clouds sat on the horizon. The wind made the sea choppy, and he had to be careful not to hit the waves at the wrong angle. Despite his hurry, Rowan seemed cautious. No point in making it away from land to wreck your boat on the way to freedom.

He was also paranoid, looking over his shoulder every so often. Bear had nowhere to hide. Most boats steered clear of each other, and they certainly didn't follow in each other's wake. Bear gained on Rowan foot by foot, and by the time they were close enough to see each other's faces, there was no denying that the chase was on.

Rowan started getting desperate. He spent half his time checking on how close Bear was, and the other half dodging sandbars, buoys, other boats, all while driving ever closer to the river. Bear would've bet money that Rowan had a car waiting for him

About ten minutes into their chase, he saw his opportunity. The Outer Banks were known for their shifting sandbars—that's what had made them so dangerous back in the day—and the Sound was no different. Some were obvious. Others, just under the surface. The only indication was a change in the color of the water. After the storm and high waves, he had to be especially careful.

Luckily for Bear, Rowan was too distracted looking over his shoulder to see what was right in front of him.

That's when Bear made his move. He gunned the boat, steering wide, coming up on Rowan's right. As predicted, the other man swerved left, trying to keep distance between him and Bear's boat. It'd be impossible to board the other vessel at this speed, but it'd be easy enough to shoot someone at such a close range. His best defensive maneuver was to make his movements unpredictable.

That worked in Bear's favor. When Rowan swerved left, he drew too close to the shallows, and the boat hit the sandbar. Rowan was thrown to the bottom of the boat as it lurched to an almost standstill, skidding over the shallows and back out into deeper water.

Bear sidled up to the *Andromeda* and cut the engine, hooking a rope to the other boat to keep them drifting together. By the time Rowan recovered from his spill, Bear was standing opposite the man.

"You gotta be more careful, man. Need any help?"

Rowan wiped blood from the gash on his forehead. "I'd say it's nice to see you again, but that'd be a lie."

Bear put his hand to his chest, mock hurt on his face. "That hurts, Rowan. That really does."

If Rowan was surprised Bear knew his real name, he didn't show it. "I take it Zeke is dead."

"I'd apologize, but I wouldn't really mean it," Bear said. "He did try to kill me first, you know."

Rowan waved the comment away. "He was a pain in the ass. He'd be dead sooner or later. You did me a favor."

"Don't expect a second one."

Rowan grimaced, and for the first time, Bear saw the stillness in his eyes. The calculation. Rowan might be smaller than him, but this wouldn't be an easy fight. Bear had come too far to make a mistake now.

"You know this doesn't end here, right?" Rowan spread his arms wide. Half his face was covered in blood now. "I might own Hatteras, but I'm just a drop in the bucket compared to what's out there. You're not cutting the head off the snake. You're just peeling away one of its scales."

Bear shrugged. "I'm just trying to protect the people I care about. Whatever else is out there doesn't concern me. The people of Hatteras deserve to feel safe in their beds at night." Bear cocked his head to one side. "I don't suppose you'd turn yourself in? Cut a deal? You could walk away from this."

"Doubtful," Rowan said. "My hands are too dirty."

"I've seen stranger things happen."

"I haven't."

The silence stretched on between them as they stood a few feet apart, eyes locked on each other. This could only end one way—one of them dead, one of them the victor. Rowan would never let Bear drag him back to shore, and Bear would never let Rowan take him from this world. From Mandy.

All the exhaustion left Bear's body, replaced by adrenaline and the will to finish this fight. He stepped close and threw a looping right hook. Rowan blocked it. Bear tossed a left jab, but Rowan dodged that, too. There wasn't much room on the boat to play defensive, but Rowan was doing a good job of it. The smaller man was trying to wear Bear down.

It wasn't going to work. Bear kept moving forward, absorbing the few blows Rowan sent his way and driving the man closer to the front of the boat. It wouldn't benefit either one of them to go in the water, but Bear would have the advantage either way. Rowan ducked and brought his fist down on Bear's forearm, right on top of his knife wound. The pain only served to intensify Bear's approach.

Rowan was faster than Bear had expected, and the second his fist came back close to his body, it shot out again, hitting Bear in the nose. His vision clouded with tears as blood poured down his face, onto his lips, and into his mouth.

Bear wanted nothing more than to wipe the snide grin from his opponent's face. So he did. He feigned left, ducked right, and then caught the other man with a left hook. A split-second later, he landed an uppercut to the man's gut, sending Rowan stumbling. Bear grabbed the back of the guy's head and drove his knee into Rowan's face. Rowan launched backward, grabbing a support pole to stay on his feet.

Bear had other plans.

Another uppercut caught Rowan on the chin. The man hovered there for a moment as though he were weightless. The light left Rowan's eyes. He fell back, and slumped over the side of the boat, halfway down to the water.

Bear stumbled a little, his muscles burning and his nose throbbing. It didn't feel broken, but it was still bleeding. He wiped the blood from his face just as a gust of wind nearly knocked him off his feet. The boat rocked. The *Andromeda* bumped into the *Serendipity*. They were drifting further now. There wasn't another vessel in sight. Bear could end this right now, kill Rowan, dump him overboard, and no one would ever know. With the *Andromeda's* motor broken, they'd assume he hit a sandbar, went unconscious, and drowned. Then Bear could drive back to shore like he'd just gotten back from a nice boat ride.

That wasn't Bear's style, as easy as it would be. He'd rather load Rowan into his boat, drive him back to shore, and bring him to justice. They had enough evidence at this point, and Bear had a feeling Ethan

Gray would be more than happy to talk. Rowan would be charged with drug trafficking and who knew what else. They might even be able to get him to turn on whoever he was working for. It could be a major bust for the local cops.

With his mind made up, Bear walked toward Rowan, still slumped over the side of the boat. The other man surged up and spun around. Bear saw a flash of orange and white before something hard hit him in the side of the head. His vision went black, and when he came to consciousness, he was lying on his back, looking up at Rowan hovering over him.

In one hand, he held a flag buoy for a crab pot, and in the other, he held the length of rope it was attached to. The arm of the flag was heavy and made of metal. Rowan was struggling to keep enough length on the line. With the weight of the pot and the wind whipping, all that pot wanted to do was sink back to the bottom of the ocean.

Rowan brought the metal arm down across Bear's knees once, twice, three times. Bear screamed in response. His vision went white with pain, and he barely registered when Rowan looped the length of rope around Bear's neck and then let go. Bear was jerked backward, toward the front of the boat. While he scrambled to peel the line away from his neck so he could breathe, Rowan pummeled him with punch after punch.

As Bear hit the front of the boat, Rowan tried to lift Bear and throw him overboard. And that was the only opening he needed. While Rowan was distracted putting all his energy into dumping Bear overboard, Bear slipped the rope from his neck and looped it around Rowan's wrist several times. He paid him in kind with the buoy as well, cracking him first across the ribs, then across the face. His jaw was offset, and just as he took a deep breath to scream in pain, Bear sent him overboard.

For a moment, Rowan kept his head above water, his eyes wide and his mouth open in a silent scream, before the pot dragged him deeper and out of view. Bear waited a few minutes to see if Rowan would reemerge.

He never did.

43

BEAR HAD ONE MORE STOP TO MAKE BEFORE HEADING HOME. BEN Carroll was where he'd always been—toiling away at his computer. When Bear knocked and he looked up, a frown creased the other man's face. He let Bear in, looking behind him as though expecting another visitor.

"Where's Zeke?" he asked, as Bear walked inside. "And why are you covered in mud? No offense, but you need a shower."

Bear laughed and settled into a chair, not caring that he left a trail of dirt. "None taken." Bear sobered. "Zeke's dead."

Ben froze, inches above his chair, before he settled into it with a sigh. "How'd that happen?"

"He tried to kill me."

"Oh. And you—"

"Killed him first."

Ben sat with that for a moment. "You're putting a lot of trust in me right now. You do remember I'm a reporter, don't you?"

Bear laughed again. "Yeah, I remember. I was hoping I could offer you a bigger story."

"Bigger than a dead body?"

"How about three dead bodies, a dirty real estate agency, and a nationwide drug trafficking problem?"

Ben's eyes grew wide. "I'm listening."

"Zeke called the cops on Reed with the intention of getting him arrested because he was going to come clean. They were both working for a man named Rowan Salazar, who's basically been running the show here on Hatteras. You ever heard of him?"

Ben shook his head. "You're saying what Zeke did to Reed was intentional?"

"He said he didn't want him to die, but he did want to shut him up."

"Guess he got his wish." Ben closed his eyes. "It's weird how knowing the truth changes nothing and everything at the same time. I used to blame Zeke for Reed's death, but I thought it was just a stupid mistake. Like he didn't think it through."

"Zeke cared more about money and drugs than his friend. And Reed's not the only person he killed. There's another Colombian native underneath a house on the canal, who washed ashore with the other from a couple days ago. They're who drove the sub that's at the bottom of the Sound."

"I got my friend on the case, by the way. He'll find it."

"Good. That'll tie the men to the sub and the sub to the house. Zeke's under there too."

"Wish I was sorry about that," Ben said. "Tragic as it is, I won't sleep any worse tonight." They sat in silence for a moment. "That's two dead bodies. Who's the third?"

"Terry Matthews, aka Rowan Salazar, the owner of the canal house and the head of the snake, at least around here. He's the one who employed Doyle. Oh." Bear grimaced. "Four dead bodies. They've probably pulled Doyle from the Murrays' house by now."

"How many skeletons do you have in your closet?" Ben asked.

"Can't tell you that, Ben." He wasn't sorry about it either. "Rowan tried to flee, I caught up with him, and he tried to kill me."

"Let me guess, you killed him first?"

"Story of my life." Bear shifted in his seat. His muscles were tired and sore, and the longer this went on, the greater his desire for a nice hot shower. It'd been too long. "He's currently tied to a crab pot out in the middle of the Sound. I'm sure someone will find him, sooner or later. And that'll tie Rowan to the house. Plus, we've got a star witness."

"Someone I know?"

"None other than Ethan Gray."

"The real estate agent?" Ben's eyebrows pinched together. "I thought he was tied up in this too."

"They threatened his kids one too many times. He's willing to talk. I told him to get a good lawyer. He might still do time, but he'll be able to expose the whole operation. At least the part centered on Hatteras. The rest of it's too big. But it'll slow them down for a bit."

"I feel like you should be prouder of yourself," Ben said. "Unless this is all in a day's work for you?"

Bear laughed. "Nice try."

"You're not going to tell me who you are, are you?"

"Not a chance." Bear liked Ben too much. "Trust me, I'm doing you a favor."

"Okay then." Ben sat forward. "You've killed two men, both in self-defense, and you're tied to two other dead bodies. Not to mention the road blowing up—"

"Also Zeke, by the way. Rosie can attest to that."

Ben shook his head, taking everything in stride. "The road blowing up, the sub full of drugs, and a real estate agency that's been bullying people out of their homes. If I dig hard enough, I'm sure I'll find money laundering too. You're handing me the biggest story of my career."

"Are you complaining?"

"I want to know what the catch is."

Bear stood and held out his hand. "All I ask is that you keep me out of it. My name, any hint to my identity, everything. Mandy and I don't exist. Forget we were ever here. Think you can do that?"

Ben stood up and clasped Bear's hand. "Yeah, I think I can do that."

44

BEAR SPENT THE NEXT TWENTY-FOUR HOURS DOING WHAT WAS NECESSARY to move on from Hatteras Island. The first thing he did was pick up Mandy and then take a much-needed shower. They spent one last night in their rent house, and Bear slept better than he had in a few months.

Then it was time for the real work to be done. They stripped the house of their belongings, packing up and putting them in the truck. Mandy was happy to move on from this place. When Bear had finished talking to the school about how she wouldn't be returning, she felt as though she could breathe for the first time since they'd arrived.

Bear was surprised Mandy didn't want to say goodbye to Jenny. The two had been close until the night of the storm, and he knew Mandy had regrets about what had happened. Even though she was sad, he was proud of her for putting that behind her. She'd come out the other side of that situation and learned a valuable lesson.

There were only three people he wanted to say goodbye to before he left. The Murrays were still in the hospital, on the mend, so Bear gave them a call to wish them a speedy recovery. They were sad to see him go, but happy that Hatteras might be a safer place to live now. They'd get enough money from their insurance to buy a new house, though it couldn't replace any of their treasured mementos. Bear sent them a check for a considerable amount of money, hoping they'd be able to finish out their life a little more comfortably.

That left Rosie. Bear had conflicting feelings about whether to say goodbye to her. The moment he decided not to walk down to the ice cream shop, was the moment she knocked on his door. He answered it with a handful of blankets in one arm and Mandy's new backpack in the other.

"So it is true," Rosie said. "You're leaving."

"Not worth me staying." He saw the hurt flash across her face. "Too much happened. Most of it wasn't good."

"But not all of it?"

He dropped the blankets and backpack in the backseat and turned to her. "Some of it was pretty nice."

"I'm sorry about everything." Rosie said. "I know I said that before, but I meant it. Every word." She took a deep breath, not breaking eye contact with him. "I did some pretty stupid things. I wish I'd known better. About Zeke. About my brother. All of it."

"I hope you can put that behind you," Bear said. "Your brother, I mean. It's not good to hold onto things."

"Is that why you move around so much?" she asked. "Always putting things behind you?"

"That's probably not good either." He chuckled. "But sometimes it feels like my only option."

Tears gathered in the corners of Rosie's eyes. "I'm going to miss you, Bear. I wish things had been different between us. I hope you can forgive me."

"I do."

"But it's not enough to get you to stay, is it?"

He didn't want to hurt her, but trust was paramount for someone who lived his kind of lifestyle. "You'll be better off without me."

"I guess I'll find out." Rosie looked beyond Bear to where Mandy stood on the front porch. "Bye, Mandy. Don't give your dad too much grief."

"I make no promises." Mandy lifted her arm to wave. "Bye, Rosie. I hope the ice cream shop does well."

The two of them watched Rosie turn around and leave. To her credit, she never looked back. Bear took that as a sign that he'd done the right thing. Maybe in another life, he and Rosie could've been together. But in this one, they both had too much baggage. Even if they were the right people, it was the wrong time.

Bear turned to Mandy. "Got everything?"

She held up a cable. "You almost forgot your phone charger."

"I was leaving that behind on purpose. Hoping this thing would die and I wouldn't have to use it."

"You sound so old when you complain about technology like that, Bear."

"I am old," he grumbled. "And you're supposed to respect your elders."

Mandy giggled. "As if."

Bear gave her his best grump face, and she laughed again as they loaded into the truck. Neither of them looked back at the house as they drove north. The road was still being repaired, but the construction crew had worked overnight to make sure one lane was open to traffic. Bear tensed as they drove by the cops on duty, but they didn't spare him a passing glance.

From there, it was a quick trip up Highway 12 and onto the ferry. When they hopped out of the truck, Mandy ran all the way up the stairs to the top deck, where they watched the setting sun hit the water in an explosion of color.

Mandy bumped her shoulder against Bear's. "I'm sorry I've been such a brat."

Bear clutched his chest in mock surprise. "What is this? An admission of guilt?"

"No!" Mandy's face turned red. "I was mad at you."

It was so rare that Mandy talked about her feelings like this. Bear didn't want to miss the opportunity. "How come?"

"I miss Sasha." Tears formed in her eyes. "A lot. And I felt so alone, like you'd already forgotten about her. Like you'd already replaced her with Rosie."

"I'll never forget her." Bear's voice choked on the emotion. He retrieved his wallet from his pocket and pulled out the only photo he had of Sasha. "See? I keep her wherever I go."

Mandy looked forlornly at the picture. "Mine was in my backpack. Now it's at the bottom of the ocean."

"That's why you didn't want to let it go that night of the storm." Bear looked down at Sasha's face one last time, then held the photo out to Mandy. "You can have mine."

"What?" She looked up at him with wide eyes. "Bear, no. Don't you want to keep it?"

"You hold onto it for me," he said. "Keep it safe."

Mandy took it and studied Sasha's face, then tucked it into a side pocket in her new backpack. She wrapped her arms around Bear. And squeezed. "Thank you."

"Oof." He laughed. "You're welcome."

Mandy wiped her tears, then looked up at him. Kids bounced back so quickly. "Where are we going next?"

"Somewhere with rollercoasters."

Mandy hadn't expected that answer. She let out a bark of laughter. "Why rollercoasters?"

"I don't know." Bear shrugged. "I feel like we could do with some more excitement in our lives."

BEAR & MANDY'S story continues in Book 3, THE LAST STOP! Order your copy today!
https://www.amazon.com/dp/B0B3RZJQP2

JOIN the LT Ryan reader family & receive a free copy of the Jack Noble story, *The Recruit*. Click the link below to get started: https://ltryan.com/jack-noble-newsletter-signup-1

LOVE BEAR? **Mandy? Noble? Hatch?** Get your very own L.T. Ryan merchandise today! Click the link below to find coffee mugs, t-shirts, and even signed copies of your favorite thrillers! https://ltryan. ink/EvG_

ALSO BY L.T. RYAN

Find All of L.T. Ryan's Books on Amazon Today!

The Jack Noble Series

The Recruit (free)

The First Deception (Prequel 1)

Noble Beginnings

A Deadly Distance

Ripple Effect (Bear Logan)

Thin Line

Noble Intentions

When Dead in Greece

Noble Retribution

Noble Betrayal

Never Go Home

Beyond Betrayal (Clarissa Abbot)

Noble Judgment

Never Cry Mercy

Deadline

End Game

Noble Ultimatum

Noble Legend

Noble Revenge

Never Look Back (Coming Soon)

Bear Logan Series

Ripple Effect

Blowback

Take Down

Deep State

Bear & Mandy Logan Series

Close to Home

Under the Surface

The Last Stop

Over the Edge

Between the Lies (Coming Soon)

Rachel Hatch Series

Drift

Downburst

Fever Burn

Smoke Signal

Firewalk

Whitewater

Aftershock

Whirlwind

Tsunami

Fastrope

Sidewinder (Coming Soon)

Mitch Tanner Series

The Depth of Darkness

Into The Darkness

Deliver Us From Darkness

Cassie Quinn Series

Path of Bones

Whisper of Bones

Symphony of Bones

Etched in Shadow

Concealed in Shadow

Betrayed in Shadow

Born from Ashes

Blake Brier Series

Unmasked

Unleashed

Uncharted

Drawpoint

Contrail

Detachment

Clear

Quarry (Coming Soon)

Dalton Savage Series

Savage Grounds

Scorched Earth

Cold Sky

The Frost Killer (Coming Soon)

Maddie Castle Series

The Handler

Tracking Justice

Hunting Grounds

Vanished Trails (Coming Soon)

Affliction Z Series

Affliction Z: Patient Zero

Affliction Z: Abandoned Hope

Affliction Z: Descended in Blood

Affliction Z : Fractured Part 1

Affliction Z: Fractured Part 2 (Fall 2021)

Love Bear? Mandy? Noble? Hatch? Get your very own L.T. Ryan merchandise today! Click the link below to find coffee mugs, t-shirts, and even signed copies of your favorite thrillers! https://ltryan.ink/EvG_

Receive a free copy of The Recruit. Visit:

https://ltryan.com/jack-noble-newsletter-signup-1

ABOUT THE AUTHOR

L.T. Ryan is a *USA Today* and international bestselling author. The new age of publishing offered L.T. the opportunity to blend his passions for creating, marketing, and technology to reach audiences with his popular Jack Noble series.

Living in central Virginia with his wife, the youngest of his three daughters, and their three dogs, L.T. enjoys staring out his window at the trees and mountains while he should be writing, as well as reading, hiking, running, and playing with gadgets. See what he's up to at http://ltryan.com.

Social Medial Links:

- Facebook (L.T. Ryan): https://www.facebook.com/LTRyanAuthor

- Facebook (Jack Noble Page): https://www.facebook.com/JackNobleBooks/

- Twitter: https://twitter.com/LTRyanWrites

- Goodreads: http://www.goodreads.com/author/show/6151659.L_T_Ryan

Made in the USA
Middletown, DE
10 February 2024

49084252R00156